An Elephant in the Garden

michael morpurgo

ILLUSTRATED BY MICHAEL FOREMAN

HarperCollins *Children's Books*

First published in hardback in Great Britain by HarperCollins *Children's Books* 2010
First published in paperback in Great Britain by HarperCollins *Children's Books* 2011

HarperCollins *Children's Books* is a division of HarperCollins*Publishers* Ltd
77-85 Fulham Palace Road, Hammersmith, London W6 8JB

This edition produced 2011 for
The Book People, Hall Wood Avenue, Haydock, St Helens, WA11 9UL

3

For videos, audio, interviews and more, visit
www.michaelmorpurgo.com

Visit us on the web at www.harpercollins.co.uk

Text copyright © Michael Morpurgo 2010
Illustrations © Michael Foreman 2010

ISBN 978-0-00-790964-3

Michael Morpurgo and Michael Foreman reserve the right
to be identified as the author and illustrator of the work.

Printed and bound in England by Clays Ltd, St Ives plc

For Bella, Freddie
and Max

Part One

Ring of Truth

1.

*T*O TELL THE TRUTH, I DON'T THINK LIZZIE WOULD EVER HAVE told us her elephant story at all, if Karl had not been called Karl.

Maybe I'd better explain.

I'm a nurse. I was working part-time in an old people's nursing home just down the road from where we live. It was part-time because I wanted to be home for Karl, my nine-year-old son. There were just the two of us, so I needed to be there to see him off to school, and be there for him when he got back. But sometimes, at weekends, they asked me to do overtime.

I couldn't always say no – we all of us had to take our turn to do weekend duties – and if I'm honest, the money helped. So at weekends, if Karl hadn't got anywhere else to go, or anyone else to look after him, they let me bring him into work with me.

I was a bit worried about it at first – whether anyone would mind, how he'd get on with all the old folks – but he loved it, and as it turned out, so did they. For a start, he had the whole park to play around in. Sometimes he'd bring a few friends. They could climb the trees, kick a football about, whizz around on their mountain bikes. As for the old folk, the children's visits became quite a feature of their weekends, something for them to look forward to. They would gather around the sitting-room windows to watch them, often for hours on end. And when it was raining, Karl and his friends used to come inside and play chess with them, or watch a film on the television.

Then, just a couple of weeks ago, on the Friday night, it snowed, and snowed hard. I had to go to work at the nursing home the next day – I was on morning shifts that weekend – and so Karl had to come too. But

he didn't mind, not one bit. He brought half a dozen of his friends along with him. They were going tobogganing in the park, they said. They didn't have a toboggan between them. They simply brought along anything that would slide – plastic sacks, surfboards, even a rubber ring. As it turned out, bottoms worked just as well as anything else. The nursing home was loud with laughter that morning as the old folks watched them gallivanting out there in the snow. In time, the tobogganing degenerated into a snowball fight, which the old folks seemed to be enjoying as much as Karl and his friends were. I was busy most of the morning, but the last time I looked out of the window I saw that, much to everyone's delight, Karl and his friends were busy building a giant snowman right outside the sitting-room window.

So I was taken completely by surprise when I walked into Lizzie's room a few minutes later and found Karl sitting there at her bedside in his hat and his coat, the two of them chatting away like old friends.

"Ah, so there you are," Lizzie said, beckoning me in.

"You did not tell me you had a son. And he is called Karl! I can hardly believe it. And he looks like him too. The likeness, it is extraordinary, amazing. I have told him also about the elephant in the garden, and he believes me." She wagged her finger at me. "You do not believe me. I know this. No one in this place believes me, but Karl does."

I hustled Karl out of the room, and away down the corridor, ticking him off soundly for wandering into Lizzie's room like that, uninvited. Thinking back, I suppose I shouldn't have been surprised. Karl was always wandering off. What did surprise me, though, was how furious he was with me.

"She was just going to tell me about her elephant," he protested loudly, tugging at my hand, trying to break away from me.

"There *isn't* any elephant, Karl," I told him. "She imagines things. Old people often do that. They get a bit mixed-up in the head sometimes, that's all. Now come along, for goodness' sake."

It wasn't until we were back home that afternoon that

I had a chance to sit Karl down and explain all about Lizzie, and her elephant story. I told him I knew from her records that Lizzie was eighty-two years old. She had been in the nursing home for nearly a month, so we had got to know one another's little ways quite well already. She could be a little prickly, and even cantankerous with the other nurses sometimes. But with me, I said, she was considerate and polite, and quite co-operative – well, mostly. Even with me, though, she could become rather obstinate from time to time, especially when it came to eating the food that I put in front of her. She wouldn't drink enough either, no matter how much I tried to encourage her.

Karl kept asking me more and more questions about her. "How long has she been in the nursing home?" "What's the matter with her?" "Why's she in bed in her room, and not with the others?" He wanted to know everything, so I told him everything...

...how she and I had taken a particular shine to one another, how she was very direct, to the point of bluntness sometimes, and how I liked that. She'd told me once, on the very first day she came into the nursing home, "I might as well be honest with you. I do not like being in here, not one bit. But since I am, and since we shall be seeing rather a lot of one another, then you may call me Lizzie."

So that's what I did. To all the other nurses she was Elizabeth, but to me she was Lizzie. She slept a lot, listened to the radio, and she read books, lots of books. She didn't like to be interrupted when she was reading, even when I had to give her some medication. She especially loved detective stories. She told me once, rather proudly, that she had read every book that Agatha Christie had ever written.

The doctor, I told Karl, thought she couldn't have eaten properly for weeks, maybe months, before she came in. And that's certainly what she looked like when I first saw her, so shrivelled and weak and vulnerable, her skin pale and paper-thin over her cheekbones, her hair creamy white against the pillows. Yet even then I could see there was something very unusual, very spirited about her – the steely look in her eye, the

sudden smile that lit up her whole fac
of her life – no relatives came to see her.
be entirely alone in the world.

"She's a bit like Gran," I told Karl, trying
her state of mind to him as best I could. "You know, like
a lot of old people, a bit muddled and forgetful – like when
she starts up about her elephant. She's goes on about it
all the time, not just to me, to everyone. 'There was an
elephant in the garden, you know,' she says. It's all
nonsense, Karl, I promise you."

"You don't know," Karl said, still angry at me. "And
anyway, I don't care what you say. I think it's true what
she told me about the elephant. She's not fibbing, she's
not making it up, I know she isn't. I can tell."

"How can you tell?" I asked him.

"Because I tell fibs sometimes, so I can always tell
when someone else is, and she's not. And she's not
muddled either, like Gran is. If she says she had an
elephant in her garden, then she did."

I didn't want to argue, didn't want to make him any
more cross with me than he already was, so I said

nothing. But I lay awake that night wondering if Karl could possibly be right. The more I thought about it, the more I began to think that maybe there *was* a ring of truth about Lizzie's elephant.

The next morning at work, with Karl and his friends cavorting about in the snow, I was sorely tempted to go in and ask Lizzie about her elephant, but it never seemed to be the right moment. It was best not to probe, not to intrude, I thought. She always seemed to me to be a very private person, happy enough in her own silence. We had got used to one another, and I think both of us felt comfortable together. I didn't want to spoil that. As I went into her room I decided that if she brought up the elephant again, then I would ask her. But she never did. She asked about Karl though. She wanted to know all about him. She particularly wanted to know when he would be coming in again to see her. She said she had something very unusual, very special to show him. She seemed very excited about it, but told me not to tell him. She wanted it to be a surprise, she said.

I noticed then she hadn't drunk anything again

from her glass of water, and told her off gently, which she was quite used to by now. I walked past the end of the bed to close her window, tutting at her reproachfully. "Lizzie, you are so naughty about your water," I told her. But I could tell she wasn't listening to me at all.

"Do you mind leaving the window open, dear?" she said. "I like the cold. I like to feel the fresh air on my face. It cools me. This place is rather overheated. I think it is a dreadful waste of money." I did as she asked, and she thanked me – her manners were always meticulous. She was gazing out of the window now at the children. "Your little Karl, he loves the snow, I think. I look at him out there, and I see my brother. It was snowing that day too…" She paused, then went on. "On the radio this morning, dear, I thought I heard them say that it is February the thirteenth today. Did I hear right?"

I checked my mobile phone to confirm it.

"Will your little Karl come in to see me today, do you think?" she asked again. She seemed to be quite anxious about it. "I do hope so. I should like to show him… I think he would be interested."

"I'm sure he will," I told her. But I wasn't sure at all. I knew full well Karl wanted to find out more about her elephant story, but it looked to me as if he was having far too much fun in the snow outside. Lizzie said nothing more about it, as I washed her, and then arranged her pillows and made her comfortable again. She loved me to take my time brushing her hair. It was while I was doing this that there was a knock on the

door. To my great relief, and to her obvious delight, it was Karl. He came in breathless, and sat down at once beside her, his face glowing, snow all over his coat, still in his hair. She reached out, brushing it away, then touching his cheek with the tips of her fingers. "Cold," she said. "It was cold on February the thirteenth, February the thirteenth…" Her mind seemed to be wandering.

"Your elephant, the elephant in the garden. You were going to tell me about your elephant, remember?" Karl said.

That was when I noticed that Lizzie was becoming quite tearful and upset. I thought perhaps Karl should go. "He can come back later, another time," I told her.

"No." She was very insistent that we stayed, that she wanted us to stay, that she had something she needed to tell us.

So I pulled up another chair, and sat down beside them. "What is it, Lizzie? Is there something about February the thirteenth that's especially important to you?" I asked her.

She turned her head away from me, unable to

control or disguise the tremor in her voice. "It was this day that changed my life for ever," she said. I reached out and took her hand in mine. Her grip was weak, but it was enough to let me know that she really did want us to stay. She was looking out of the window, and pointing now.

"Look, do you see? Do you hear? The wind is blowing through the trees. The branches, they are shaking. Are they frightened of the wind, do you think? Little Karli said it that day, that the trees were frightened of the wind, that they wanted to run away, but they couldn't. We could, he said, but they couldn't. He was very sad about it." She smiled at Karl. "Karli was my little brother, and you remind me so much of him. And this makes me happy, that you are here, I mean; and on this day too, so that I can tell you my story, our story, Karli's story and mine. But it makes me sad also. On February the thirteenth I am always sad. The wind in the trees, it makes me remember."

I had noticed before that she spoke English in a strange way, pronouncing her words carefully, too

correctly, and in proper sentences. Her name might have been English, but I had always thought she might be Dutch, or Scandinavian, or German perhaps. "It was a hot wind, a scalding wind," she went on. "I do not believe in hell, nor heaven come to that. But if you can imagine it, it was like a wind from the fires of hell. I thought we would burn alive, all of us."

"But you said it was in February," Karl interrupted. I frowned at him, but Lizzie didn't seem to mind at all. "That's in wintertime, isn't it?" Karl went on. "I mean, where were you living? Africa or somewhere?"

"No. It wasn't in Africa. Didn't I tell you this before? I think I did." She was suddenly looking a little unsure of herself. "There was an elephant in the garden, you see. No, honestly there was. And she liked potatoes, lots of potatoes." I think my wry smile must have betrayed me. "You still do not believe me, do you? Well, I cannot say that I blame you. I expect you and all the other nurses think I am just a dotty old bat, a bit loopy, off my rocker, as you say. It is quite true that my bits and pieces do not work so well any more – which, I suppose, is why I am in here, isn't it? My legs will not do what I tell them sometimes, and even my heart does not beat like it should. It skips and flutters. It makes up its own rhythm as it goes along, which makes me feel dizzy, and this is not at all convenient for me. But I can tell you for certain and for sure, that my mind is as sound as a bell, sharp as a razor. So when I say there was an elephant in the garden, there really was. There is nothing wrong with my memory, nothing at all."

"I don't think you're batty at all," said Karl. "Or loopy."

"That is very kind of you to say so, Karl. You and I shall be good friends. But I have to admit that when I come to think of it, I cannot remember much about yesterday, nor even what I had for breakfast this morning. But I promise you I can remember just how it was when I was young. I remember the important things, the things that matter. It is as if I wrote them down in my mind, so that I should not forget. So I remember very well – it was on the evening of my sixteenth birthday – that I looked out of the window,

and saw her. At first she just looked like a big dark shadow, but then the shadow moved, and I looked again. There was no doubt about it. She was an elephant, quite definitely an elephant. I did not know it at the time, of course, but this elephant in our garden was going to change my life for ever, change all our lives in my family. And you might say she was going to save all our lives also."

2.

$\mathcal{L}$IZZIE PAUSED FOR A MOMENT OR TWO, THEN SMILED ACROSS at me sympathetically, knowingly. "No, no, you are too busy for this, dear, I can see that," she said. "You have to get on. You have other patients to look after. I know this. I was a sort of nurse once. Nurses are always busy. But I can talk to Karl. I can tell him my elephant story."

There was no way I was going to miss her story now. If Karl was going to hear it, then I was too. And the truth was that I had already sensed from the tone in her voice that she was making nothing up, that Karl had been right about her. "You certainly can't stop now," I told her. "I'm off duty at twelve, and that's just about now. So I'm on my own time."

"And we want to know all about the elephant, don't we, Mum?" said Karl.

"Then you shall, Karli. I think from now on I shall call you Karli, like my little brother. So it will be as if you are inside the story." She laid her head back on her pillows. "I have had quite a long life, and quite a lot has happened, so it may take a little while. You are going to have to be patient. I think to begin with you have to know names and places. I was called Elizabeth then, or Lisbeth some people called me – I became Lizzie much later. Mother, we always called Mutti. And I had a little brother, as I have told you, about eight years younger than me, little Karli. He was always full of questions, endless questions, and when we answered, there'd always be another question, about the answer we'd just given. 'Yes, but why?' he would ask. 'How come? What for?' In the end we would often become impatient with him, and just tell him it was 'for a blue reason'. He seemed happy with that – I do not know why.

"Karli was born with one leg shorter than the other,

so we had to carry him a lot, but he was always cheerful. In fact he was the clown in the family, kept us all laughing. He loved to juggle – he could do it with his eyes closed too! The elephant loved to watch him. It was as if she was hypnotised. The elephant was called Marlene. Mutti got to name her because she was working with the elephants in the zoo. She named her after a singer she loved, that many people loved in those days. Marlene Dietrich. I wonder if you might have heard of her – no, I don't suppose you have. She's been dead a long time now. She was very slim and elegant, and blonde too, not at all like an elephant, but that did not seem to matter to Mutti. She called the elephant Marlene, and that was that.

"We had a gramophone at home, a wind-up one with a big trumpet – you do not see them like this any more, only in antique shops – and so Marlene Dietrich's voice was always in the house. We grew up with that voice. She had a voice like dark red velvet. When she sang it was as if she was singing only for me. I tried to sing just like her, mostly in the bath,

because my singing sounded better in the bath. I remember Mutti would sometimes hum along with her songs when we were listening to them. It was like a kind of duet."

"But what about the elephant?" Karl interrupted again, not troubling much to hide his impatience. "I mean, how come this elephant was in your garden in the first place? Where were you living? I don't understand."

"Yes, you are right, dear," she said. "I was getting ahead of myself, rushing on too quickly." She thought long and hard, collecting her thoughts, before beginning again.

"It would be better perhaps if I start again, I think. A story should always begin at the beginning. No? My own beginning would be a good start, I suppose...

So, I was born on the ninth of February nineteen twenty-nine, in Dresden, in Germany. We lived in quite a big house, a walled garden at the back, with a sandpit and a swing. And we had a woodshed where there lived the biggest spiders in the whole world, I promise you! There were many high trees, beech trees, where the pigeons cooed in summer, right outside my bedroom window. At the end of the garden was a rusty iron gate with huge

squeaking hinges. This gate led out into a big park. So, in a way, we had two gardens you might say, a little one that was ours, and a big one we had to share with everyone else in Dresden.

Dresden was a wonderful city then, so beautiful, you cannot imagine. I have only to close my eyes and I can see it again, just as it was. Papi – this is what we all called our father – Papi worked in the city art gallery restoring paintings. And he wrote books about paintings too, about Rembrandt in particular. He loved Rembrandt above all other artists. Like Mutti he loved listening to the gramophone, but he preferred Bach to Marlene Dietrich. He loved boating best of all, though, and fishing too, even more than Rembrandt or Bach. At weekends we would often go boating on the lake in the park, and in summer we would take a picnic and the gramophone with us, and we would have a picnic by the shore, a musical picnic! Papi loved musical picnics. Well, we all did.

Every holidays, we would take a bus into the

countryside, to stay with Uncle Manfred and Aunt Lotti on their farm – Aunt Lotti was Mutti's sister, you understand. We would feed the animals and have more picnics. Papi built a tree house for us on an island out in the middle of the lake – which was more like a large pond than a lake, when I come to think about it – and it was fringed all around with reeds, I remember, and there were always ducks and moorhens and frogs and tadpoles and little darting fish. We had a small rowing boat to get across to the island, and plenty of trout to fish for in the stream that ran down into the little lake – so Papi was happy.

Sometimes when the harvesting was done, we'd all be out there in the field of stubble long into the evenings, gathering the last grains of golden corn. And whenever we could on summer nights, Karli and I would sleep up in the tree house on the island. We would lie awake listening to the gramophone playing far away in the farmhouse, to the owls calling one another. We would watch

the moon sailing through the clouds.

We loved the animals, of course. Little Karli loved the pigs especially, and Uncle Manfred's horse – Tomi, he was called. Karli would go riding on Tomi with Uncle Manfred every day out around the farm, and I would go bicycling on my own. I went off for hours on end. I loved freewheeling down a hill, the wind in my face. It was our dreamtime, full of sunshine and laughter. But dreams do not last, do they? And sometimes they turn into nightmares.

I was born before the war, of course. But when I say that, it sounds as if I knew there was going to be a war all the time I was growing up. It was not like that, not at all, not for me. Yes, there was talk of it, and there were many uniforms and flags in the streets, lots of bands marching up and down. Karli loved all that. He loved to march along with them, even if the other boys used to taunt him. He was so small and frail, and suffered greatly from asthma. They'd call him 'Pegleg', because of his limp, and I hated them for that. I would shout at them, whenever I felt brave enough that is. It was not only the mockery in their faces and the cruelty of their words that I hated so much, it was the injustice. It was not Karli's fault he had been born like that. But Karli did not want me to stand up for him. He used to get quite angry at me for making a fuss. I do not think he minded about them nearly as much as I did.

I think I have always had a strong sense of justice, of fair play, of what is right and what is wrong. Maybe it is just natural for children to be born like this. Maybe I got it from Mutti. Who knows? Anyway, I always recognised injustice when I saw it, and I felt it deeply. And believe you me, there was plenty of it about in those days. I saw the Jews in the streets, with their yellow stars sewn on to their coats. I saw their shops with the Star of David daubed in paint all over the windows. Several times I saw them beaten up by Nazi stormtroopers, and left to lie in the gutter.

At home, Papi did not like us to talk about any
of this, about anything political – he was very strict
about that. We all knew about the terrible things
the Nazis were doing, but Papi always told me that
our home should be an oasis of peace and
harmony for us in a troubled world, that it only
made Mutti angry or sad or both to talk about it,
and that little Karli was far too young anyway to
understand about such things. Besides, Papi would

say, you never know who's listening. But down on the farm on our holidays one summer – the summer of nineteen thirty-eight it was – Mutti and Papi, Uncle Manfred and Aunt Lotti, got into a long and heated argument. It was late at night, and Karli and I were already upstairs in bed. We heard every word of it.

Uncle Manfred was banging the table, and I could hear the tears of anger in his voice. "Germany needs strong leadership," he was saying. "Without our Führer, without Adolf Hitler, the country will go to the dogs. Like Hitler himself, I fought in the trenches. We were comrades in arms. My only brother was killed in the war, and most of my friends. Is all that sacrifice to be for nothing? I remember the humiliation of defeat, and how people starved in the streets after the war. I was there. I saw it with my own eyes. Make no mistake, it was the government in Berlin, and the Jews, who betrayed the Fatherland and the army. And now Hitler is restoring our pride, putting things right."

I had never in my life imagined Uncle Manfred could be this angry. Mutti was furious too, and called him 'ein dumkopf' – in English this means a fool, or a fathead. She was saying that Hitler was a madman, that the Nazi regime was the worst thing that had ever happened to Germany, that we had many dear friends who were Jews, and that if Hitler went on the way he was going, he would lead us all into another war.

Uncle Manfred, who was ranting now, and quite beside himself, replied that he hoped there would be a war, so that this time we could show the world that Germany had to be respected. Then, to my utter surprise, mild-mannered Aunt Lotti joined in, calling Mutti 'nothing but a coward and a lousy Jew-loving pacifist'. Mutti told her in no uncertain terms that she was proud to be a pacifist, that she would be a pacifist till the day she died. Through all this, Papi was doing his best to try to calm things down, and said that we were all entitled to our own opinion, but that we were all family, all German, and that we should stick together, whatever our views. No one was listening to him.

The argument raged on for most of the night. To be honest, at the time I didn't understand much of what they were talking about – only enough to know that I was on Mutti's side. Karli understood even less, but we were both so upset and surprised to hear them being angry with one another, and shouting like that. When I think about it now, I realise I should have been more knowledgeable about what they were saying. But I wasn't, not then. I was just a teenage girl growing up, I suppose. Yes, I hated all the dreadful things I'd seen the stormtroopers doing in the streets, but the truth is – and I am ashamed of this now – that I was far more interested in boys and bicycles, than in politics – and more in bicycles than boys, I have to say.

I do not think I understood just how serious the argument had really been, till the next morning. When Karli and I came downstairs into the kitchen for breakfast, Mutti had all the cases packed. She was in tears, and Papi announced grim-faced to Karli and me that we were going home. He said that Uncle Manfred and Aunt Lotti had decided we were no longer welcome in their house, and that we wouldn't be seeing them or speaking to them ever again. Uncle Manfred and Aunt Lotti were nowhere to be seen. I shall never forget walking away down the road from the farm, knowing we'd never be coming back. Karli started crying, and very soon I found myself doing the same. It felt like the end of a wonderful dream. And that is exactly what it turned out to be. Only a year or so later, Papi came home one day in his grey army uniform, and told us they were sending him to France. It came as a total surprise to me. That was how the war began for us, the beginning of our nightmare, of everyone's nightmare."

3.

"MAYBE I WILL HAVE THAT DRINK OF WATER NOW," LIZZIE
said, reaching for her glass. I was only too pleased to
hand it to her.

"I think you're tiring yourself," I told her.

"I am fine," she replied firmly. "Quite fine. Just a dry
throat, that is all."

"What about the elephant?" Karl asked her. "You
haven't told us about the elephant yet."

"Patience, patience," Lizzie said, laughing. "You are just
like Karli, just like him. Questions, always questions. The
likeness between you is – how is it you say it? – uncanny.
I was just coming to that part of the story." She took a
deep breath, and closed her eyes before she went on.

"This was about the time Mutti went to work in the zoo, with the elephants. With so many men away at the war, the women were doing more and more of the men's work these days. And anyway, now that Papi was gone, I suppose we must have needed the money. Papi came home every few months on leave, but each time he seemed to me to be more and more changed, a different man almost. He was thinner in the face, with dark rings under his sunken eyes. He would be sitting in his chair, Karli on his knee, and hardly saying a word. We never went boating together. Papi didn't go fishing. He did not even listen to his beloved Bach on the gramophone. And he never laughed, not even at Karli's tricks and antics.

Then, as the war dragged on, year after year, Papi came home less and less. We heard he was in Russia somewhere, but we never knew exactly where. We had letters of course, but not that

often. Whenever a new one did come, Mutti would read it out loud to Karli and me every evening before bedtime. We would have then what Mutti always called a 'family moment' together, holding hands around the kitchen table and closing our eyes to think of Papi. Then she would put the letter up with all the others on the mantelpiece, behind the photo of Papi in his uniform. The mantelpiece became like an altar to his memory.

Karli would often ask us if Papi was dead in the war. Of course not, we told him. Papi was

fine. He would be home soon, we told him. We told him anything to keep him happy, that it would all be over before we knew it, and everything would be back the way it had been. But as the war went on, hiding the truth was becoming impossible. The news worsened with every passing week. Food became scarce. More and more cities were being bombed all over Germany. We had more and more days off school because there was not enough coal any more to heat the classrooms. The Russian Army, the Red Army we called it, was closing in on us from the east. Refugees were flooding into Dresden. And the Allies, the Americans and the British, were already marching into Germany from the west. More and more husbands and sons and brothers were being reported dead or missing. It was common now every week, for one of our schoolfriends to learn the dreadful news that a father or a brother was not coming home. So of course Mutti and I began to fear the worst for Papi. We both feared it, I know we did, but did not dare speak of it.

We used to listen to the radio every evening, Mutti and I. All through the war we had done this, listening for news from the particular battlefront where we thought Papi was fighting. They still tried to make bad news sound like good news – they were very good at that. But no matter what they told us, we knew, as everyone did by now, that the war was lost – that it was only a question of how quickly it would end, and of who would get to us first, the Red Army from the east, or the Allies from the west. We all hoped it might be the Allies – from the refugees we had heard such terrible things about the Red Army. In the end it was just too painful to listen any more to the radio, so we didn't. We listened to the gramophone instead, and longed every day for the war to be over, for Papi to be home again with us. Every night before we went up to bed, Mutti would make sure that Karli and I said goodnight to Papi's photo. Karli liked to touch it with his fingertips. I had to lift him up

because he was still too small to reach it himself.

I think I was often angry in those days – with the way the world was, I mean. And I am ashamed to say that sometimes I took it out on Mutti, blaming her for just about everything. I have no excuse for this, except that I was fifteen, and felt that day by day all my happiness was being taken from me. I felt hollow inside, empty, and angry. It is difficult to explain, but I felt as if I was all alone in the world, a world I used to love, and that I had come to hate. More and more I felt apart from everyone and everything, from my friends and family even, as if I no longer belonged. Like Papi, I could no longer even take pleasure in Karli's playfulness. He went on joking and juggling just the same, with the world falling apart about us. I became more and more irritated with him, and with Mutti too. Mutti could see this, I think, and became all the more maternal and attentive towards me, which only made things worse, of course.

We did not live far from the zoo where Mutti

worked, so that in the dark of the evening, if I went out into the garden, I could hear the lions roaring, and the monkeys chattering and the wolves howling. I had taken to getting out of the house whenever I could. However cold it was, I would sit on the swing and listen to them. I would close my eyes, and try to imagine myself out in the jungle away from everything that was going on, far from the war and all this unhappiness. One evening Mutti came out to join me, bringing me my coat.

"You'll catch your death, Elizabeth," she said, wrapping the coat around my shoulders. She began to tell me all about the animals we were hearing, their names, the countries they had come from, their personalities, who was friends with who, all their funny habits. And then she started talking about Marlene again, the young elephant she had almost adopted by now. I just didn't want to hear about Marlene. Mutti was talking on and on about her with such deep affection, almost as if she really was part of her family. It occurred to

me then, quite suddenly, that maybe this elephant was more precious to her than me and Karli.

It was some years now since Marlene had been born, four or five maybe. Mutti had been there at the birth, and she was so proud of that, and prouder still when the *Herr Direktor* at the zoo said that since she was the one who saw her come into the world, then she should be the one to name her. After that it was almost as if Marlene was her baby. And in the last few days in particular, she had been talking about her all the time because she was very worried about her.

Only a month or two before this, Marlene's mother had become sick, and had died quite suddenly. So Mutti would be home late each evening, spending even longer hours now at the zoo, just to be with Marlene, to comfort her. Elephants grieve just like we do — Mutti had often explained this to us. She told us that Marlene needed her to be there with her as much as possible, that she had been off her food and depressed ever since her mother had died. And now there was a photo on the mantelpiece of them both together, Mutti stroking Marlene's ear. It was right next to the photograph of Papi, and his letters, and I didn't like that at all.

Mutti had taken Karli and me with her into the zoo to see Marlene many times. It was true, she did seem sad and dejected. And Mutti was right, she was the sweetest elephant in the world, so gentle. She had such kind eyes. Her trunk seemed to have a life all of its own, and she rumbled and groaned almost as if she was talking, which always made Karli giggle. And whenever he giggled, that seemed to cheer Marlene up a lot. Karli and that elephant became the best of friends. It was the highlight of Karli's life when Mutti took us in to see Marlene. They were so alike, those two – Marlene and Karli, I mean. Naughty, inquisitive, funny. Karli would talk to her as he fed her, as he led her about by her trunk. Like the best of friends, the best of soul mates they were.

If I am honest I think I was a little jealous, and maybe this was why I was heartily sick of hearing Mutti going on and on about her confounded elephant. And here she was doing it again.

"Do you hear that, Elizabeth?" she said, grasping my arm. "It is Marlene! I am sure that is Marlene trumpeting again. She hates to hear the wolves howling. I've told her that they won't harm her, but she is all alone at night, when I am not there, and she gets frightened. Do you hear her?"

"For goodness' sake, Mutti!" Even as I was shouting at her, I knew I shouldn't be. But I couldn't stop myself. "There is a war on, Mutti, or hadn't you noticed? Papi is away at the fighting. He's probably lying there dead in the snow in Russia right now. In the city there are thousands of people starving in the streets. And all you can talk about is your precious Marlene. She is just an elephant, a stupid elephant!"

Mutti turned on me then. "And if I talk about

the war, will it bring Papi home? Will it? Will the bombing stop? Will the Russians and the Americans turn round and go home? I do not think so, Elizabeth. We are losing this war, and do you know what? I don't care. What can I do about it? Why should I talk about it? How can that help? All I can do is look after my children and look after my animals, and I will do both, to my dying breath. To Marlene, I talk about you and Karli. To you, I talk about Marlene. Is that so terrible?"

I had never seen her like this, and at once regretted my cruel words. We cried then, and clung to one another in the dark of the garden. It is strange how a moment like that can change things around. Until then, I had simply been her child, her daughter, and she my mother. Until then, we had confided in one another very little. Suddenly, we were opening our hearts to each other. This was when she told me what it was that had been troubling her so much.

"For weeks now, I have not been sleeping at nights, and do you know why this is, Elizabeth?" she said. "It is because I should be worrying about Papi, and you and little Karli. And I do, I do. But not enough, and this makes me feel so bad. There is always something else I am thinking about because it is terrible, so terrible that I cannot put it out of my mind."

"What, Mutti, what?" I asked her.

She led me away from the house then, to the garden bench set against the back wall – the bench where she and Papi always used to sit on summer evenings when they wanted to be alone. Karli and I used to watch them from our bedroom window, and always wonder what they were saying. Sometimes, I remember, little Karli would pretend to smoke, mimicking everything that Papi did, until he had us both in fits of laughter. I think it was the first time I had ever sat there on the bench with Mutti. I was in Papi's place, and it felt very special.

Mutti held my hand tight as she talked to me. "The *Herr Direktor* at the zoo, Elizabeth, he called us in together, all the keepers, everyone – this was a month or two ago. He told us he had something very serious to tell us. Until now, he said, Dresden has not been bombed. Almost all the big cities in Germany lie in ruins: Berlin, Hamburg, Köln. Thousands upon thousands are dead. Only Dresden has been spared. But sooner or later, he told us, the bombers are sure to come, and so we have to plan for this. So far we have been lucky, but our luck cannot last for ever. Why should Dresden be special? When the bombers do come, we are well prepared. We all have basements or shelters to go to, and they are deep, so deep that many of us will have a good chance to survive. We know where to go. We have all done our air-raid drill. But the animals, he said, have nowhere to go, nowhere to hide. If the zoo is hit by the bombs – and in a raid this is very likely – then it is possible that many of the animals might escape from their cages and find their way into the city. The authorities say this cannot be allowed to happen."

"What will they do with the animals then?" I asked her. "Will they take them away to somewhere safe?"

"I am afraid not," Mutti replied. "The *Herr Direktor* told us that very regrettably, it has been decided that we must destroy most of the animals, especially the big carnivores, the lions and tigers and the bears, and also the elephants — any animal that might be a threat to the people in the city. I know this is a dreadful thing to have to do, he told us, but if the worst comes to the worst and the bombers do come, then we shall just have to do it. We have no choice. We should prepare ourselves. That is what the *Herr Direktor* said, Elizabeth," she cried, almost in tears by now. "To prepare ourselves! How can I prepare myself to stand by and watch them shoot Marlene? Tell me that. I cannot bear the thought of it, Elizabeth. I just cannot."

"And will the bombers come, Mutti?" I asked
her.

She did not reply at once. "I am afraid so,
Elizabeth," she said. "If I am honest – and I think
you are old enough for me to be honest with you
– I can see no reason why they should not come.
Sooner or later they must come. We all know
this."

I think I had never been so frightened in all
my life as I was at that moment. Mutti tried to
comfort me all she could.

"I should not have told you, I should not," she
whispered, holding me close. "But do not worry.
Whatever happens, I shall look after you and little
Karli. The air-raid sirens will give us plenty of
warning, and the shelter is very near, isn't it? And
it is so deep that the bombs cannot reach us down
there. We have practised it so many times. We
shall survive this, I promise you. You, me, and
little Karli. They can send all the bombers they
like, and we will survive. And I make you another

promise, Elizabeth. I shall make sure also that Marlene survives with us. I will not let this war take from me all those I love." She wiped away my tears then, as she held me at arm's length, brushing the hair from my eyes. "Believe me, all will be well, Elizabeth. Now let us go inside, and say our goodnights to Papi."

So that is what we did. In the morning all three of us found ourselves together in Mutti's bed. Mutti said she had slept better that night than for a very long time. At breakfast, she told us that from now on that is how she would always like us to sleep – together. She was happier than I'd seen her in ages, and so was I. As we left the house that morning, she kissed me goodbye, and then whispered something in my ear as she hugged me. "I have had an idea, Elizabeth, in the night, a wonderful idea, a grand idea. A secret."

"What?" I asked.

But she would not say any more.

On the way to school with Karli that day, I

heard the sudden throbbing drone of planes overhead. I felt a warm shiver of fear crawling up my back. Then Karli was leaping up and down, and waving wildly.

"They're ours!" he cried. "They're ours!" And they were too. This time."

Part Two

Ring of Fire

1.

IT SEEMED TO ME, AS I WAS LISTENING TO LIZZIE, that she was living every moment of the story again in her head, even as she was telling it. But the effort had been too much, and had clearly left her feeling exhausted. She laid her head back on her pillow, and was silent for a while.

"Maybe that's enough for now, Lizzie," I told her, getting up to go, and encouraging Karl to do the same. "You can tell us the rest another time, tomorrow maybe. Come along, Karl." I could see Karl was not at all pleased with me. He didn't argue as such, but darted me one of his darkest looks.

"Stay," she whispered, holding out her hand. "Please

let him stay. You want to know what Mutti's secret was, don't you, Karli? And now is the right moment to tell you. It is better today because tomorrow will be too late. Tomorrow it will not be the thirteenth of February any more. That is why I must tell you what happened now. It is the anniversary, you see. There is a time for these things. And besides," she went on, looking at me a little mischievously, and meaningfully too, "besides, as you know, for someone my age, tomorrow may never come. Sooner or later we all run out of tomorrows. This is true, I think. No?"

"Don't talk like that," I said, knowing full well I was beaten. "You've got plenty of tomorrows left. Now, are you quite sure you're not too tired?"

"I will be tired when my story is finished, dear, and not before," she replied.

"All right then," I told her. "We'll stay, but only if you drink some more water for me. Is it a deal?" I was only half joking, and she knew it.

"Your mother, Karli," Lizzie said, with a smile, "she is a most excellent nurse, and I am sure she is an

excellent mother too, but she can be rather bossy sometimes. Am I right?"

"Yep," Karl replied, nodding vigorously, and grinning triumphantly all over his face.

"It is a deal," Lizzie said. And she drank a few more delicate sips, before dabbing her lips with her sheet, and settling back on to her pillows.

"It is strange," she began...

"We were so preoccupied, I think, by the ordinary things in life, that after a while I did not give much thought to Mutti's mysterious idea. I did ask her about it once or twice, and she said she was 'working on it'. I certainly did not forget her warnings about the bombers that might soon be coming, nor about the armies closing in on us from all sides. How could I? I just tried my very hardest not to think about it.

Looking back, it is hard to believe now, that I was not terrified all the time. But I was not. Life went on as normal. Karli and I went to school, as normal – when there was enough coal to heat the place, that is. There was homework to do, and tests. People walked and talked in the streets, as usual. The trams rattled by, as usual. I could not forget the war – of course not, none of us could – but I suppose we all just had to put it to the back of our minds, and get on with living each day, getting through as best we could. Maybe that was the only way of keeping our hopes alive, by looking beyond all we were seeing around us, and the shadow of disaster that hung over us. I hoped so hard that Mutti was right, prayed every night that all would be well, that in a few days the war would be over, that the bombers would not come, that I would look down the street one morning and see Papi come walking home, and I would run to him and he would hold me in his arms again. And when the spring came, we would all go to see Uncle Manfred and Auntie Lotti down on the farm, and we would be friends as

we were before, and Karli and I would sleep in the tree house and watch the moon riding through the clouds, and everything would be just as I remembered it, just as it should be.

The snow came, as it has today, and of course little Karli loved that. He was the only one at school who could juggle snowballs! We went sledging in the park, built a snowman in the garden, threw snowballs at one another on the way to and from school. And the whole city seemed to be sleeping silently under its blanket of snow. The pipes froze. We froze. It was the coldest winter I had ever known. Very soon the snow was not so much fun any more. It just made life more wretched for everyone, particularly for the refugees in the streets. Every day now I would see them in their hundreds, outside the soup kitchens, lining up in the snow, or huddled together against the cold in doorways, the children crying. And the war dragged on, miserably, interminably.

My sixteenth birthday was on the ninth of February nineteen forty-five, a day I shall never forget, and not because I had lots of presents, or lots of friends to the house for a party. There was no money for that, and besides, no one was in the mood to celebrate anything. Mutti and Karli had made me a birthday card, and gave it to me at breakfast. I remember it was a kind of collage, full of cut-out pictures of circus life, with clowns and acrobats and jugglers and horses, and elephants, of course, lots of elephants. I put it up on the mantelpiece behind Papi's photograph before we went off to school that morning.

When we got home in the evening, Mutti was not there. This did not surprise us. We had got used to her being late home these days. But on this particular evening she was even later than usual. I was beginning to get a little worried, when I heard the garden gate squeaking open. Then Mutti was calling to us from the garden. She was coming in through the back way. I

thought it was a bit strange, but did not think anything more about it. I was just relieved she was home. She came in the back door, stamping the snow off her boots. She was carrying a sack over her shoulder.

"Potatoes," she said, dumping the sack on the floor, and sitting herself down heavily at the kitchen table. She was breathless and glowing from the cold, and happy too, as happy as I had seen her in a long time. "I shall make a potato soup for your birthday, Elizabeth, with a little ham – I have a little ham left. I shall make you the best potato soup a mother ever made for a daughter. And... and, I have a present for you, a surprise."

"A surprise?" I said.

"Of course," she laughed. "You can hardly have a birthday without a surprise, can you? And I promise you it'll be the biggest surprise you ever had too! It is outside in the garden. I think it is maybe a little bit too big to bring inside."

Karli got to the window before I did, which irritated me, because to my mind this was my birthday – my surprise, not his. I pushed him out of the way. I could see it was still snowing outside, but at first I could see very little else. By now Karli had rushed to the back door and opened it. "There is an elephant in the garden, Mutti!" he cried. "Why is there an elephant in our garden?"

Then I saw her too, a huge shadow that moved and became an elephant, as it came towards me into the light from the window. Mutti had her arms around me and was kissing the top of my head.

"My secret, remember?" she whispered. "Happy birthday, Elizabeth."

"It is Marlene!" cried Karli, leaping up and down in delight.

"Is that really her?" I said. I was still not sure whether my eyes were deceiving me or not.

"It took a while to persuade the *Herr Direktor*,

but in the end I managed it," Mutti told me. "I told him the truth, that if anything happened to her, it would break Karli's heart. And I also convinced him that Marlene needed me night and day now, that without her mother she might well just pine away and die of sadness. I had to be there with her all the time. And that is true, quite true. I'm sure of it. Even better, I got him to promise me that Marlene will be spared if the other animals have to be shot, if the bombers come. She might be big, I told him, but she is still only young, gentle as a kitten and no danger to anyone. He was not at all easy to persuade, but as you know, I can be very insistent. From now on, Marlene will be coming home with me from the zoo every evening, and I shall take her back to the zoo in the morning. We shall not let her out of our sight. She lives with us, like one of the family. So, for your birthday, Elizabeth, you have a new little sister. Well, a big sister, I suppose."

"And she is my sister too!" cried Karli, beside himself with excitement. I remember the exact words he used then. *"Wunderbar! Ausgezeichnet!"* Wonderful! Excellent!

I had no words. I think I was still too amazed to think of any.

"Tonight," Mutti went on, "we will all have potatoes. Marlene loves to eat potatoes. She loves to be hand-fed, doesn't she, Karli? Remember? And now we can all do that, can't we? She eats a lot of potatoes, but the good thing is that she doesn't seem to mind eating the half-bad potatoes, the ones people won't eat."

As we ate our steaming potato soup that night, Marlene eyed us through the window, the end of her trunk exploring the glass. Afterwards, we went outside in the snow, and Karli reached up, took her by the trunk and led her into the woodshed, which was half empty, so there was plenty of room for her to shelter inside from the snow. He stood beside her stroking her ear and

feeding her potatoes as if he'd been doing it all his life, talking to her all the while. And Marlene talked back too, in her own way. No, she did, she really did, groaning and grunting and rumbling – she had a whole language of her own!

I held the lamp for Mutti as she shook out some straw around Marlene's feet. But I did keep my distance from Marlene. Maybe it was because she was just so huge to be near to – she seemed much bigger somehow in our woodshed than she had back in the zoo. But I think I was nervous also because she had a way of looking at me that I found quite uncomfortable, at first. She was not looking at me, so much as right into me. So I knew she must be able to see the lingering jealousy I was still feeling about her and Karli. But then I began to understand that she wasn't judging me. No one had ever gazed into my eyes quite like this before. I can only describe it as a look full of curiosity, kindness and love. Any lingering resentment I might have still been harbouring against Marlene vanished during that first night in the woodshed.

When we heard the wolves howling from the zoo in the distance, and she began to look unsettled and anxious, I reached out and stroked her trunk, to comfort her, and to show her that whatever she felt about me, I felt the same. I remember Karli looking up at me in the shed, and saying, "Now I have two sisters, one with a long nose and one with a shorter one – well, only a little shorter!"

I will not tell you what I said to him, but it was not polite!

Neither Karli nor I slept much that night at all. We knelt side by side by the window looking out at the woodshed. All we could see of Marlene was the dark bulk of her inside the shed. And then, just occasionally, her trunk would reach out into the snowy night.

"She is catching snowflakes, isn't she?" Karli said.

We were the kind of family who generally kept ourselves to ourselves. We liked it that way, and as Papi had often said, in those times it was safer that way too — always best not to draw attention to ourselves. So until now, our neighbours down the street had taken very little notice of us. But the next morning, all that changed. There was a startled face at almost every window in the street as we walked out of the back gate and into the park, Mutti leading the elephant by the trunk on their way to the zoo, and Karli and I, satchels on our backs, tramping along behind them through the snow, taking the short cut to school. Some of our schoolfriends who saw us, now joined us in the park, dozens of them, until there was a whole cavalcade following along behind, all of them full of questions, and high with excitement.

When we came to the parting of the ways, we all stood and watched Mutti and Marlene walking away through the trees in the direction of the zoo, before running off down the hill to the school. That day at school no one talked about the Red Army or about the war. We all of us had something else to talk about. Marlene, we soon discovered, had made Karli and me famous overnight. I remember how important it made me feel to be surrounded by a crowd of admirers. It wasn't a feeling I had experienced that much before, and I liked it. And I could

see, in playtime, that Karli was also enjoying the limelight just as much as I was. What with his juggling, and all his other fancy tricks, he was more used to being the centre of attention than I was. No one called him 'Pegleg' any more, I noticed. He was 'Elephant Boy' now, and that was fine by him. That evening we threw snowballs at one another, and larked about and laughed all the way home.

A RATHER WORRIED-LOOKING POLICEMAN DID COME to the house later that same evening to question Mutti about the elephant we were keeping in our garden. But Mutti was expecting just such a visit from the authorities, and had thought of everything. She read him out a letter from the *Herr Direktor* of the zoo, giving his permission, and declaring that the elephant was a young one, only four years old, recently orphaned and so needed special care and attention, that she was an unusually calm elephant, and quite safe to be left under the supervision of Mutti overnight; that he had inspected the garden himself, and there was no danger whatsoever to the public. The policeman

wanted to read the letter himself, and even then he still wanted to check that the garden where Marlene was being kept was secure. So we took him out there to show him, Karli leading the way.

Marlene was sheltering in her shed. The policeman didn't want to get too close, I could see that. He walked across the garden and rattled the gate to satisfy himself that it was safely shut. But he said we should chain it up, just to be sure. When he turned around he found Marlene was right there in front of him. She had come to introduce herself. She did this by reaching out her trunk to touch his face. He looked very alarmed at this, but when a few moments later Marlene's trunk happened to knock off his cap, and we all laughed, he had to laugh too.

After that, he went away happy, leaving us happy too, and relieved that Marlene was now officially allowed to stay. And Karli, in particular, could not stop giggling about the policeman's hat being knocked off. Later, it became one of those family stories we all went on telling, but Karli told it best – mimicking the shock on the policeman's face wonderfully well.

After that first day, with Mutti bringing Marlene home every evening, everyone wanted to come and have a look at the orphan elephant in the garden. And all our friends suddenly wanted to come to see us – some of them were friends that until then we never knew we even had. Inquisitive faces were for ever peering through the bars of the garden gate. Marlene loved all this adoration, and Karli did too – he was always out there in the garden with her, making quite sure everyone knew that Marlene was his own personal elephant. Marlene loved it when people offered her titbits. She'd take anything: stale breadcrusts, cabbage leaves, even an apple or a bun sometimes, but I think she was always hoping for potatoes – as Mutti said, they were her real passion. So whenever anyone appeared at the gate, Marlene would always wander over with Karli and accept their offerings only too willingly.

There was a problem with all this, quite a big problem actually – apart from the fact that we seemed

to be open house now to the whole neighbourhood –
and that was that very soon huge piles of elephant
dung began to appear in the snow all over the garden,
like giant molehills they were.

"Wonderful for the vegetable garden," Mutti said.
We carted it away in barrowloads to a pile in the corner
of the garden. Karli seemed to love doing this –
anything to do with Marlene, he loved – but I hated it.
You cannot imagine how much there was of it, nor
how smelly it was. It was hard, I discovered, to push a
wheelbarrow and hold your nose at the same time!

It was a few days before I plucked up enough
courage to go out into the garden to see Marlene on
my own. She came out to meet me from her
woodshed, wandering slowly towards me, snuffling at
the snow with her trunk as she came. She rumbled at
me contentedly from somewhere deep and echoing
inside her, and then explored my hair and face with the
tip of her trunk – her way of saying hello. When I
reached up to stroke her ear, I think she hoped I had
brought her a potato. I would have done so too, if I

had thought of it. But she did not seem too disappointed. We let our eyes do most of the talking, I remember. We stood there with the snow coming down around us, each of us knowing, I was sure of it, that we were making a friend for life. I did sense in her eyes the depth of the grief she was still suffering after the loss of her mother. And without my ever saying anything, I knew she understood all my own fears, about Papi, about the bombers that might come any day now, about the war.

Marlene was always so accepting and so patient. I never once saw her irritated or angry, until the day the dog came that is. It was a big dog, a loud dog – an Alsatian, I think, but I can't be sure. This dog would appear suddenly at the garden gate, and bark at her, his whole body shaking with fury. He kept coming back again and again, and every time Marlene would run at him across the garden, trumpeting, tossing her ears, flapping them, but that only infuriated the dog even more. We all tried to drive him off, rattling a stick at him through the bars of the gate, and shouting at him

to go away – Karli hurled some dung at him once – but none of it was any use. Sooner or later that wretched dog always came back.

Then one evening the dog's owner was there with him at the gate, the dog barking his head off as usual. We could hear that Marlene was becoming frantic again, and Karli was out there, shouting at him to clear off. So Mutti went running out into the garden, and I followed her. She told the man that enough was enough, that his dog was out of control and frightening the elephant. They had a heated row through the bars of the gate, and the man went away swearing and shaking his fist, shouting at us that the

park was a public place, that his dog had every right to bark, and that elephants belonged in zoos anyway.

Mutti went on fuming with indignation about him all evening. All during supper and afterwards, she kept getting up to look out of the window to check on Marlene. I could see she was becoming very anxious about her. In the end, she went out to see her in the garden.

"She is still pacing up and down out there," Mutti said, as she came back inside. "She does that in her cage at the zoo whenever she is feeling unhappy about something. That horrible dog has really upset her. I shall take her for a walk. That usually settles her down. I think that is what she needs. There is a lovely full moon out there. Will you come with us, children?"

The truth is, I didn't want to. I was warm where I was, and certainly did not want to go out there into the cold again. But of course Karli hardly needed an invitation. He already had his boots on, and was shrugging himself into his coat. "Can I hold her trunk, Mutti?" he cried. "She likes me to hold her trunk."

They were halfway out of the door already by now.

I only went with them because I did not want to be left behind. I grumbled about it, I remember. "Do we really have to?" I moaned. But no one was listening to me. I made sure I was going to be as warm as I could be. I pulled my hat down over my ears, wrapped my scarf around me, and then grabbed Karli as he was going out of the door, and did the same for him, put on his hat and scarf because he hadn't bothered. He hated me fussing over him. He just wanted to get out there and be with Marlene.

Moments later we were through the gate and out into the park beyond, the snow bright with moonshine, and the whole world silent and peaceful about us. Karli was leading Marlene by her trunk, making his usual clicking noises and telling her to gee up, just like he had always done with Tomi back on Uncle Manfred's farm. I noticed again something I had often noticed before, that when Karli was at his happiest, he limped much less. He was stomping on ahead of us through the snow with Marlene, and there was scarcely a sign of a limp at all.

Mutti put her arm through mine as we walked. "Wherever Papi is, it is the same moon for him, Elizabeth," she said. "Maybe he is looking up at it, right now, like we are."

That was the moment the dog came bounding out at us from under the trees, barking wildly. I saw at once it was the same Alsatian that had been tormenting Marlene through the gate. Mutti was running at him, clapping her hands and shouting at him, but the dog would not be put off, would not go away. Instead he circled round behind Marlene, snarling and growling

at her. That was what made Marlene suddenly whirl around to face him, sending Karli sprawling into the snow. I ran to him at once and helped him to his feet. By the time I looked up again, Marlene was charging off through the snow, chasing the dog away, trumpeting as she went, her trunk flailing, her ears in full sail. And Mutti was stumbling after her, calling for her to stop. But I could see that there would be no stopping Marlene now, until she had either chased the dog out of sight, or had trampled him to death.

3.

I TOOK KARLI BY THE HAND AND WE BOTH FOLLOWED Mutti, running through the snow after Marlene. But the snow was deep and we soon tired, and were reduced to a walk. Ahead of us the chase went on. However hard the dog tried to bound away over the snow and escape, Marlene kept after him. All the while her trumpeting was echoing through the park, and louder now in my ears than seemed possible – until I began to realise that it was not Marlene's trumpeting I was hearing at all, but the sound of the air-raid sirens wailing over the city. I stopped to listen, to be quite sure my ears were not playing tricks on me.

Karli gripped my arm. "An air raid!" he cried. "An

air raid!" All I knew then was that we had to get to the shelter fast, as we had been taught. Ahead of us, Mutti too had stopped in her tracks. She was yelling out to Marlene to come back. Again and again she called, but Marlene just kept going. She was almost out of sight now in amongst the trees, as Mutti came stumbling back towards us.

"There is nothing more we can do for now, children," she said. "We shall find her later. We must get home, to the shelter. Come quickly!" She grabbed Karli's hand.

"No!" Karli cried, pulling away from her and turning to run. "No! We can't! We can't leave her. We have to catch her! I'm going after her. You go home if you like. I'm not coming."

"Karli! Karli, don't be silly! You come back here this minute, do you hear me?" Mutti was shouting after him, shrieking almost; but I could see it was pointless, that Karli had made up his mind. I started running after him then, so did Mutti. But he was already way ahead of us, and Marlene was by now no more than a shadowy shape moving through the trees, and then I lost sight of her altogether. We were catching Karli up fast, when, and not for the first time, he staggered, and fell to his knees, exhausted. Mutti and I were trying to help him up, doing all we could to persuade him that we had to get back to the shelter. He was still protesting, still struggling against us, fighting us, when we heard the sound we had been dreading for so long.

The bombers.

The bombers were coming. It sounded like a distant humming at first, then it became a droning, like a swarm of bees, a swarm that was coming closer, ever closer. We looked up. We could still see no planes. We could not tell from which direction they were coming because they seemed to be all around us, but invisible. Then, in no time at all, the sky above us was filled with a thunderous throbbing roar, so loud that I thought my ears might burst. Karli had his hands over his ears and was screaming. And then the bombs began to fall, behind us, on the city, on the far side of the park, on where we had come from, our street, our house. The

whole world shuddered and shook with every blast. To me it felt like the end of the world had come.

Now we had no choice. We all of us knew at that moment that there could be no going back. Mutti picked Karli up in her arms. He clung on and buried his head in her shoulder, crying out for Marlene. And we ran, we ran and we ran. We did not know tiredness any more. Fear alone kept our legs running. I looked up once more, and saw the planes flying across the moon. There were hundreds of them up there. By now the bombs were falling all over Dresden. We heard the whine of them falling, the crump and crunch of them, saw the flash of explosions, saw fires raging everywhere.

There was no more argument, not about Marlene, who had disappeared into the night by now, and not about returning home to the shelter. Marlene we could do nothing more about, and it was obvious that if there was any way of escaping the bombs, it would be in the open country ahead of us beyond the suburbs, not in a shelter back in the burning city.

It was the city they were bombing, not the countryside. We only had to keep going, I told myself. We would soon be out of the park, into the outskirts of the city, closer all the time to the safety of the fields and the woods beyond.

We tried not to, but we had to stop from time to time, to catch our breath. And whenever we did, we

would stand there, gazing back at the city. Our city it was, and it was being destroyed before our eyes. Searchlights crisscrossed the sky. Anti-aircraft guns were firing, firing, pounding away. But the planes just kept on coming, the blast of their bombs ever nearer, ever louder, roaring in our ears. The flames from burning houses and factories were licking high into the sky, leaping from one building to the next, from one street to the next, from one fire to another, each fire, it seemed to me, seeking out another fire to be with, so it could become an inferno, so it could burn more furiously.

Time and again we turned away from it and ran on, partly because the heat was so intense, and partly because we could bear to watch no longer. We were out of the park by now, out on to the road through the suburbs. A sudden wind was getting up, a strong fierce wind that gusted in our faces as we walked. We leaned into the wind and staggered on through the snow.

We followed the road to the top of a steep hill, and by then Mutti could carry Karli no further. She had to stop. We found ourselves on our knees in the snow, looking back down at the city, at the ring of fire that now encircled it entirely. Kneeling there, we heard quite distinctly through the drone of the bombers, the sound of shooting. And we could hear screaming. One look at Mutti's horrified face, and I knew this screaming for what it was, the shrieking of animals, of dying animals, and that it came from the direction of

the zoo. They were shooting the animals. Mutti put her hands over Karli's ears, and hugged him to her. She wept then, uncontrollably, as much in anger as in grief, I thought. Karli and I put our arms around her to do our best to comfort her. There we knelt, the wind searing hot on our faces now, while the shooting went on, and the bombs fell, and the city burned.

In the end it was neither Karli nor me who brought her comfort. Instead it was the sound of breathing close behind us, and then, miraculously, Marlene's trunk winding itself around us, enfolding us. That was a moment I remember so well, because all three of us burst out laughing, laughing through our tears. We had gone looking for Marlene, lost her, and now she had found us. We were on our feet at once, overjoyed, Karli kissing her trunk again and again, and Mutti stroking her ear, but telling her how naughty she had been to run away like she had. I looked up into Marlene's face, and saw the fires of the city burning in her troubled eye. She knew what was happening, understood everything. I was sure of it.

I think it was Marlene's sudden unexpected reappearance that gave us all fresh hope, new strength, Mutti most of all. "Well, children," she said, brushing the snow off her coat, "we have no house to go back to, and certainly there will be very little left of the city. So I have been thinking. There is only one place we can go to. We shall go to the farm, to Uncle Manfred and Aunt Lotti. It is a long, long way to go on foot, but there is nowhere else."

"But you and Papi," I said. "You told us we could never go back to the farm, not after…"

"I know," Mutti told him. "But we have no choice, have we? We shall be needing food, shelter. They will look after us, I know they will. It was a family row we had, that is all. I am sure everything is forgiven by now, and that we can all put it behind us. When we get there, they will welcome us in with open arms. It will be fine, I promise you. You will see."

"Elizabeth?" Karli said, his hand stealing into mine. "Elizabeth? Why do they do this terrible thing? Why have the bombers come?"

"Because they are our enemies, and because they hate us," I told him. "And because they are brutes. To do this they must be brutes, the Americans, the British, all of them."

"But why do they hate us?" he asked me.

Mutti answered for me then, and I was glad she did because I had no answer to give him. "If they hate us, Karli," she said, "it is because we have also bombed their cities. What we are seeing now is a world gone mad, children, a world full of brutes, all intent on killing one another. And we should not forget that we are all responsible for making it happen, for letting it happen."

As we turned and walked away, we had to cling on to one another, so that the wind did not blow us back towards the city, towards the fire – the gusts of wind were so strong. I remember Karli looking up at me, and pointing at the trees. "The trees in the gardens, they are shaking, Elizabeth," he said. "I think they are frightened of the wind. They want to run away like we are, but they cannot. Why is the wind blowing so hard?

Why is it so angry?" Not even Mutti had an answer to that. Karli was crying then, crying for our burning home, and maybe also for the trees we were leaving behind, that could not run away.

So began our long trek through the snow, along a road that was quickly becoming ever more clogged with dozens, hundreds, then thousands of others like us, streaming out of Dresden, all of us desperate to leave the city behind us. When I looked back – and I tried not to – Dresden was no longer a city any more. Rather, it looked to me like one vast bonfire, where fire

caught fire with fire, a fire whipped up by a mighty wind of its own making, that buffeted our faces, that was doing all it could to stop us from escaping, all it could to suck us back into the burning city. There was the stifling stench of smoke all about us. Karli was finding it difficult to breathe sometimes, and kept having to stop to cough the smoke out of his lungs.

Mutti and I were worried that it might bring on one of his asthma attacks, but thankfully it did not. And still the planes came. Still they dropped their bombs.

That was the longest night of my life. I had never before witnessed human misery on such a scale. It is the sound of a people in despair that I shall never forget: the weeping, the sobbing, the screaming and the praying. How fast we all wanted to get out of the city that night, and how slowly we were moving. We shuffled forward through the cold and the dark, most of us on foot, but many on bicycles, in cars, lorries, farm carts, everyone jostling to find some way to get ahead, to move just a little faster. So many were desperate to find someone dear they had lost, and so many were wrapped in bandages and were crying out in their pain.

It was like a walk through hell, and it seemed never-ending. Only the military convoys and ambulances were able to find a way through, honking their horns at us, waving us all aside. We longed with every moment to be out of the blazing suburbs and into the welcome darkness of the countryside. Everyone on that road knew that there was safety in that darkness. I think that was all that kept us going.

All night long we trudged on, but as the hours passed, the road became even more congested – mostly refugees, on foot like us, but many more now, it seemed, pulling carts loaded up with old people or children, their possessions piled around them. As the growl of the bombers at last died away, the air was filled with whimpering. It was as if the whole world was in mourning. By first light there was the shuffling of feet to be heard, and creaking cartwheels and occasionally a neighing horse. Looking back over my shoulder from the top of a hill, it seemed to me like a gigantic funeral procession.

It was mostly one-way traffic. But at dawn, more convoys of trucks filled with soldiers came roaring past on their way back into the city, motor-cycle outriders waving us frantically to one side. They were the first to take any notice of Marlene, some of them pointing at us and staring, as they passed us by. As for our fellow refugees, maybe they had been too dazed, too traumatised, or just too tired, to pay much attention to this young elephant that was wandering along with them. A few of the children were curious, but everyone, including the children, was subdued. There were no smiles of excitement amongst them, only a dull amazement.

I have no idea how far we walked that first day of our long march – probably only a few kilometres, but it felt like a hundred. We had no food, no water, only the snow by the roadside to eat. And progress was still painfully slow. We were simply a part of a long wretched trail of refugees that was filling the road ahead of us and behind us as far as the eye could see. Sometimes the road became so jammed we could scarcely move at all. That was the worst of it. We seemed to be getting nowhere. Arguments were breaking out. Tempers were fraying.

Karli, though, seemed quite happy to be tramping alongside Marlene, holding her trunk and talking to her all the time. He did not once complain, about his leg, about his wheezing, about the cold. I wish I could say the same for myself. My feet were in agony, my ears ached, and I was longing for something to eat,

anything. When I mentioned any of this to Mutti, which I did, often, she would just put her arm around me, and say with a gently reproving smile and a shrug, "Me too, Elizabeth, me too." It did not help, it did not make me feel any better.

Sometime in the afternoon of that same day – we were walking along a road through a pine forest, I remember, and were making even slower progress than ever – Mutti suddenly took Marlene by the ear, and without any warning, led us off down a forest track away from the road. The walking was at once more difficult here, the going more arduous, the snow deeper, but at least we weren't dragging along with hundreds of others, being endlessly held up. Karli kept asking her why we were going this way. I did too, but Mutti wouldn't answer.

"Just keep walking," she told us. Some of the other refugees back down on the main road were shouting out after us, telling us we would get lost in the forest. Mutti paid them no attention, but just walked on without answering, without even looking back. "I don't want any of them following us." she said. "We're better off on our own."

After a while, once we were well out of sight of everyone on the road, she stopped and told us what she had in mind. "Papi and me, children, when we were young, when we were first married, before you two came along, we used to cycle all the way from the city out to Uncle Manfred's farm. On the main road it was a very long way round. Papi was good with maps, and he discovered this short cut. So after that we always came this way. On our bicycles it was a whole day's hard ride. On foot I think maybe we could do it in two, but we must not stop. We shall get too cold if we stop. Best of all, children, there is a stream only a couple of hours ahead, where Papi and I used to sit and have a picnic. We may not have the picnic, but we can drink all the water we like, can't we? We will just have to imagine the picnic, that's all. And maybe we shall find a house somewhere, and can beg some food, you never know. One thing is for certain, we were never going to find

either food or water back down on that road. And travelling that slowly, it was going to take us for ever to get to the farm. We may have a bit of a hard slog ahead of us, children, but we shall manage. We have got to, haven't we? And once we get to the farm, we will be warm as toast, and we shall have all the food we can eat. You remember how Aunt Lotti piles the plates? And there'll be hay in the barn for Marlene. All our troubles will be over, you will see."

The thought of a drink of water, and the hope of food, must have given new strength to my aching legs. I strode on ahead up the snow-covered track. I heard the stream before I saw it, a great rushing torrent tumbling down off the hillside and into a pool of bright water. I could see it was iced over in places. The water was freezing of course, but we didn't mind one bit. Marlene stood in the pool and drank there right with us, sloshing her trunk about in the water, loving every moment of it, as we were too.

Here, for the first time, we could forget for a few

moments everything that had happened. But once we were walking on again through the forest we soon fell silent and thoughtful. None of us I think could forget the burning city we had left behind us, the suffering we had witnessed on that long march. And we could still smell the smoke – it seemed to be clinging to the trees all around us, drifting about us like a yellow mist.

Karli was breathless now, stumbling ever more often, wheezing and coughing almost constantly. We were becoming more and more worried about him. I told Karli I would carry him, so did Mutti, but Karli would have none of it. He insisted on staying with Marlene, on walking alongside her, holding her trunk, and there was no arguing with him. But walking side by side behind him now, Mutti and I could see that his wheezing was becoming worse all the time.

It was my idea, and all these years later, I am still quite proud of it. "When I was little, before the war, Mutti," I said. "I went on elephant rides in the zoo, didn't I? You took me, didn't you, before you worked

there? So Karli could ride up on Marlene, couldn't he? Why not?"

"I thought of that, but it is no good," Mutti replied. "It was only the older elephants that were used for rides, and they have to be properly trained. And besides, Marlene is still too young. She has never in her life had anyone on her back. I have no idea how she would take to it."

"It is worth a try, Mutti, surely," I argued. "Karli cannot go on like he is."

"Maybe you're right. And it is in Marlene's blood, that is for sure," Mutti conceded. "I mean, her mother used to give rides in the zoo for years, till she got sick."

Moments later – and, as you can imagine, we had no arguments from Karli about this – we were lifting him up, and sitting him there astride Marlene's neck. Much to Mutti's relief and mine, it did not seem to bother Marlene in the least. She just flapped her ears a little, and groaned quite contentedly. With Karli riding now – and he was as happy as he could be about that of course – he was very

soon wheezing less. As for Marlene, she plodded on through the snow as if she had been giving rides all her life.

Somehow, the water I had drunk at the stream had managed to satisfy my hunger as well as my thirst. By the time the dark of night came down around us, it was no longer hunger that bothered me so much, as the cold. I had by this time lost all feeling in my feet and hands, but now the intense cold seemed to be seeping into my whole body, and chilling me to the bone. Time and again I begged Mutti to stop. All I wanted to do was to curl up in the snow and go to sleep for ever. It was only Mutti that kept me moving that night. Time and again she had her arm around me, helping me on, and every so often she would whisper words of encouragement. "Every step you take, Elizabeth, you are nearer to the farm, nearer to food and a warm bed," she would say. "Just remember that, and put one foot in front of the other. That is all you have got to do, and we shall get there."

To be honest I cannot remember a great deal about the rest of that long and terrible night. I do know that at one moment we seemed to come out of the trees and out on to the open hillside. Here we heard again that sound we all feared so much – the air-raid sirens, a distant rumbling and then the roar of approaching bombers. In no time they were right over our heads.

"What are they bombing?" cried Mutti. "Can they not see there is no city left to bomb? All they are bombing is fire."

We stood there on that bleak hillside, quite unable to take our eyes off the huge fireball that was rising now over the city. No words could speak our horror, no tears could cry our sorrow. Even Karli had no more questions. We were some distance away from the city, but I could feel the warmth of that great fire on my face as I watched. I felt it shivering some of the cold out of me, and I have to admit they were shivers of pure pleasure.

But I was at once overcome with guilt. I was

thinking about what a terrible thing it was, that while I was basking in the heat of it, many thousands of people must still be trapped in the city, some of them my own friends from school. I thought of them down in their shelters, and wondered if any of them could possibly survive such a raging inferno as this. Mutti turned me away from it. "This is the last time we look back, Elizabeth," she said. "From now on, we only look forward." So we left the city to burn and went on our way.

There was one more incident I do remember about that night, and it makes me ashamed to tell you about it. But I will tell you because I want you to know the story as it happened, not simply as I would have wished it to happen. No matter how often I begged Mutti to stop and give us a rest, Mutti would not listen. The more she refused, the nastier I became. In the end she lost her patience, and turned on me. "What do you want, Elizabeth?" she cried. "Do you want us to freeze to death out here? Do you? The farm is only a few hours away, twelve kilometres, maybe less. Now get a grip of yourself and just walk."

I was angry back at her, hysterical almost, saying all manner of things I should not have said, about Papi going off and leaving us, about how parents always ruin the lives of their children. She took me in her arms then, and hugged the anger out of me, telling me how much Papi loved me, and she loved me, and how we had to survive to be there for Papi when he came home. Karli, I remember, looked down on us, bewildered, from high up on Marlene.

So as the bombs fell and Dresden was destroyed, we walked away, on and on, no strength left for arguing any more, no strength left even for speaking. The next morning, a grey-pink dawn it was, the growing light soft on the snow, we came down from the hills into the valley, a valley we knew and loved so well. And there below us we could see the farm where Uncle Manfred and Aunt Lotti lived, the familiar farmhouse with the barns and sheds all around, and beyond them the lake, now frozen over,

and the island in the middle, our island. We had known such despair and sorrow during the night, and found such joy in the morning.

Marlene quickened her step noticeably, and, following along behind, so did we. She knew we were nearly there, and this was hardly surprising, I suppose, since Karli was whooping and waving up there on her back, and Mutti and I were laughing out loud in our relief. I noticed from some way off that there seemed to be no animals outside, but then I knew that was only natural. We had been there often enough in the winter, for Christmas a few times, and I remembered that Uncle Manfred kept his animals inside during the worst of the winter months. But all the same, the place did look strangely deserted.

Mutti spoke my thoughts exactly. "There is something wrong, I think," she said. "Aunt Lotti, she keeps that stove of hers going all the time, winter or summer, I know she does. There is no smoke coming out of the chimney."

As we came across the snow-covered fields, and

past the frozen lake, flocks of crows lifted off, most of them from the poplar trees out on the island cawing at us, cackling at us, angry at our intrusion. But they were the only sign of life. I ran on ahead of the others and opened the farmyard gate. The snow had drifted up against the front door of the house. There were no footprints in the yard, not one. A quick look told me that all the sheds were empty. Tomi was not in his stable. No chickens warbled

from inside the hen-house. Mutti knocked at the door, and called out again and again. No one answered. No one came.

I left them, and walked around the back of the farmhouse towards the hay-barn, where Karli and I had played so often, leaping from the top of the stack to the bottom into piles of soft sweet hay. That was what I was thinking of, as I opened the barn door. It was dark inside, so I pushed it wide open to let the light in.

There was a man lying stretched out in the hay, a man in a uniform, an unfamiliar blue uniform. He looked fast asleep, or dead – I was not sure which. Mutti was there beside me suddenly, and Karli too. Marlene came wandering in after them, and wasted no time at all, before reaching up with her trunk, tugging at the hay, and stuffing it into her mouth. The sound of her grinding jaws was loud in the silence. "Who is he?" Karli whispered.

"That is the enemy, Karli," Mutti said. "An airman. From one of the bombers that has destroyed our city. British. RAF." She reached for a nearby pitchfork, gripped it tight in two hands, and advanced slowly towards him."

Part Three

Ring of Steel

1.

$\mathcal{L}$IZZIE BROKE OFF FROM HER STORY, AND TURNED TO LOOK AT us. "I'm so cross with myself. I meant to bring my photograph album with me," she said. "But I left it at home in my little apartment when they brought me here. I miss it so much. I used to look at it almost every day, you know. The things I could have shown you. There is a photo of us all down on the farm, when I was a small girl, and Karli was even smaller, just a baby in Papi's arms – in happier times. I love that photo. We are all outside that same hay-barn, and I am sitting up on Tomi, with Mutti holding him, and I have long plaits and a big gappy smile – my two front teeth are missing. Uncle Manfred must have taken the picture because he is not in it, and Aunt Lotti is looking very serious as usual. When I look at this photo I can see it all so clearly. I can almost breathe in the air of the countryside. And I have a photo also of Marlene, only one, but mostly it is of her trunk because she was trying to eat the camera! It is enough though. Sometimes I worry that everything that happened might be some kind of a dream, or that maybe I have made the whole thing up. But I only have to look at those photographs to know I did not, that it really did happen. I wish I had brought them with me. I wish I could show you."

"We could always go and fetch them, if you like," I said. "If you trust us with your key, that is."

"Of course I do, dear," she replied. "After all, I am trusting you with my story, aren't I? I have never told

anyone else, you know. That would be kind, very kind. I have the key to my apartment here, in my drawer, Karli. You might have to wiggle the key in the lock a bit, but you will manage. You can find it easily enough. Just around the corner from Main Street, on George Avenue, the first house. You go up the steps. Number two." She was reaching towards her bedside cupboard as she spoke, but hadn't the strength to pull open the drawer. So Karl did it for her, searching around till he found them. There was an elephant on the keychain.

"To remind me," she said, smiling. Then she noticed something else in her drawer, and her eyes brightened suddenly. "Ah, now this I never leave behind, Karli. I never go anywhere without it. Can you pass it to me? This is what I wanted to show you."

I had no notion at first as to what it might be, and from the look of puzzlement on his face as he handed it over to her, neither did Karl. It was a small, round object, made of metal, black in colour. "It's very heavy, and cold too," Karl said. "What is it?" By now I was beginning to think I recognised it for what it was.

"A compass?" I said. "Is that what it is?"

Lizzie was cradling it lovingly in her cupped hands, and for several moments seemed too overcome to speak.

"You are quite right, dear," she replied at last. "This is a compass, to help you find your way. But this is not just any old compass. It is the best compass in the whole wide world, I promise you. Because it has shown me the way all through my life." She opened the lid, and touched the face of it with her fingertips. "I first saw this compass on that day," she went on, "the day we found him lying there in the barn..."

"I think sometimes that perhaps I had two beginnings in my life; the moment of my birth, of course, and the moment I set eyes on this man, this airman who I knew had bombed my city, a bomber,

a killer, who had caused so much suffering to so many. As Mutti had said, here was the enemy, close to, in the flesh.

He was not the first I had seen. Several times I had watched columns of prisoners-of-war being marched along the streets in Dresden. To be honest, I had never taken that much notice. They looked much like our soldiers, only dirtier, sadder. Some people would scream obscenities at them, and spit at them, and throw things, so I would look away. It made me feel ashamed. I never thought people could be that angry, that vindictive. I could not imagine what would make them do such things. But for just a moment, looking down at him lying there in the hay in Uncle Manfred's barn that morning, I understood it completely, and I hated him, and I hoped he was dead. Then he opened his eyes and looked at me, and I knew right away that he was no more of a killer than Papi was.

I often wondered afterwards what it must have been like to wake up and see the four of us staring down at him, Mutti with the pitchfork pointing at his chest, and Marlene towering over us, her trunk reaching down towards him. His eyes were wide with alarm, as he sat up in the hay, and raised his hands in the air.

"English?" Mutti said. Her voice was shaking, from anger, I thought, more than fear.

"No… nein," he replied. "Canadian. Canada. Canada."

"Bomber?" Mutti was holding the pitchfork at his throat now. "RAF?"

The man nodded.

"England, America, Canada, it does not matter where you come from. Do you know what you have done? Have you any idea?" Mutti was shouting at him now, and crying too in her fury. "Did you see the fire you made? Are you proud of that? Do you know how many you killed? Do you care? Do you have any idea how beautiful a city Dresden was before you came? Do you? I should kill you, kill you right now."

Mutti raised the pitchfork. I really thought she was going to do it.

I grabbed her arm, and held it fast. "You cannot do it, Mutti!" I cried. "You must not! How often have I heard you say it? To Papi, to me, to Uncle Manfred and Aunt Lotti. All killing is wrong, no matter what. It is what you always told us. Remember?"

It was many long moments before Mutti lowered the pitchfork. Then she stepped back, and handed it to me. "Maybe I cannot do it," she said. "But I wanted to. That is what your bombs do. They make hate. I think at this moment I hate you more than I have ever hated anyone in my whole life."

"I do not blame you." To our astonishment, the airman was speaking to Mutti in almost perfect German. "I saw the fire from the plane. I could not believe it. I did not expect it to be like that, that the whole city would burn like that. None of us did."

"Oh, really?" said Mutti. "So tell me, what did you think it would be like then, some kind of a carnival, a firework display perhaps?"

"We thought it would be like the blitz on London, I suppose, when the *Luftwaffe* came." The airman replied softly, not responding at all to Mutti's fury. "I was there. And that was terrible enough. But last night it looked like the fires of hell. That's what we're doing in this war, all of us, on your side, on our side: we are making a hell on earth, and we do not seem to be able to know how to stop. I am sorry. I know that is not enough, but it is all I can say."

No one spoke for some time, until Karli piped up, breaking the silence between us. "Do you really fly a Spitfire?" he asked.

"No, only a Lancaster, I'm afraid. And I didn't fly it anyway. I'm not a pilot, I'm a navigator." And when he smiled then, I remember thinking that he looked more like a boy than a man.

"And you navigated your way to Dresden so you could drop your bombs on thousands of innocent people," said Mutti. "Well, bravo you! How do people like you sleep at nights? That is what I want to know." Mutti was looking about her, suddenly

nervous. "And the others? Where are the others of your crew? Are you alone?"

"All dead," the airman replied. "We were hit by flak over the city. Everyone in the plane was killed, except for Jimbo – he was the pilot – and me. Jimbo told me to get out right away, to jump. He said that he would hold the plane as steady as he could, and then follow me. But he never did. I saw the plane blow up as I was parachuting down. He saved my life. And that's funny, you know, because Jimbo and me, we never got on, not really. Bit of a joker, he was, thought it was all just one big game – the war, I mean. Him and me, we'd have big arguments. He turned out to be a pretty good buddy after all, didn't he? They were all good buddies, and they're all gone now."

"Don't you dare expect me to feel sorry for them," Mutti said, not so threatening towards him as she had been, but still angry at him. "Not after what they did, what you did. And how come you speak German anyway?"

"I have a Swiss mother," the airman told her,

"and a Canadian father. So I grew up speaking German and English."

Karli was not concerned at all with any of this. He was full of his own questions. Mutti kept trying to stop him from speaking to the airman, but Karli ignored her. He wanted to know the man's name.

"Peter," the airman said. "Peter Kamm."

Karli wanted to know how old he was.

"Twenty-one," came the reply.

Then Karli took it upon himself to introduce everyone. "I am Karli, and I am nine years old. This elephant is called Marlene, and she is from the zoo in Dresden, and she is four years old, and I am the only one who is allowed to ride on her. And this is Elizabeth. She is sixteen, and is always telling me what to do. And Mutti is... well, she is Mutti. And I am hungry. Are you hungry, Peter?"

Mutti took him by the arm and pulled him away then. But Karli could not stop looking at the young man, and the truth was, neither could I. I think I must have done nothing but stare at him the whole

time. Now that he had a name, I found I was not looking so much at the uniform any more. He was much taller than I expected when he got to his feet.

Pitchfork in hand again, Mutti ushered him out through the barn door. We left Marlene shut in there, helping herself busily to the hay, and rumbling with pleasure.

It was not difficult to break a window and let ourselves into the farmhouse. Mutti said she felt bad about having to do it, but that needs must. We could hardly stand out in the snow and wait, could we? She would explain it all later to Uncle Manfred and Aunt Lotti, when they came home, she said. They would understand. I was not so sure that they would. The stove was out, but it was still warm, so we thought they could not have been gone that long. Things were in a mess too, as if they had left the place in a hurry. The more we looked around the more we were sure that, like so many others, they had left to join the great exodus westwards, taking with them what they could.

Luckily for us, Uncle Manfred and Aunt Lotti must have left in too much of a rush to take all their food with them. There were some rounds of cheese – Uncle Manfred always made his own – and we found some fruit in jars, and pickles too, and some honey. But best of all, down in the cellar Mutti discovered a whole ham. I got the fire going in the stove. Karli fetched in the wood from the shed. And all the while, the airman sat at the kitchen table, forbidden to move by Mutti, who kept a fearsome eye on him – and she took the pitchfork with her, I noticed, wherever she went around the house.

When he offered to help me with the fire, she snapped at him, and told him to sit where he was and be quiet. Karli and I were under strict instructions from her not to talk to him at all, even when we were sitting down with him to eat at the kitchen table, but that did not stop us from sneaking a look at him from time to time as he was eating – he was obviously as ravenous as we were. So we all ate in silence, not a word being spoken between us

– until, that is, Mutti left the kitchen, telling us she was going to check on Marlene out in the barn. Before she went out, she handed me the pitchfork, and told me to use it if I had to.

I hate silences between people, I think I always have. I was longing to say something to Peter while Mutti was out of the room, but I was too shy, and anyway I could not think of a thing to say.

Karli was never shy though, never backward in coming forward. Before I knew it, he had got down from the table, and was juggling, with two large fir-cones he'd found on the windowsill.

"Can you do this?" he cried.

"My little brother likes to do tricks," I explained to Peter. "He likes to play the fool. He is a bit of an actor, I suppose."

"I can see that," Peter said. "He reminds me of me, when I was little. It is what I used to do back home in Canada. Acting, I mean. It was all I ever wanted to do, go on the stage, like my mother before me, and my father. I had just got started in Toronto, and then all this happened. Anyway, it will be over soon enough now, and when it is, I'm going right back there. I can't wait.

I liked to listen to him talk. He was so full of spirit, so determined. The truth was that I was enjoying his company, even though, of course, I knew that I should not be. The thing was, you see, that I could tell he liked being with me, talking to me, looking at me. I think maybe that is why I felt at once so much at ease with him. When you are young, and you find for the first time that someone likes you like this, it is powerful. Very powerful.

But Karli soon had Peter's attention again, with his wretched juggling. Four fir cones now. He was getting ambitious. A few minutes later, when Mutti came back in again, she found Peter and Karli sitting cross-legged on the floor in front of the stove, deep in conversation. Peter had something in his hand and was showing it to Karli, who was fascinated by it. I couldn't quite make out what they were saying, or what it was, but I was busy at the sink by now, and not paying much attention. Mutti shouted at Karli to get up and come to her at once.

"Look, Mutti!" he said, ignoring her completely. "Peter has a compass. He says it is like magic. He's been telling me all about it. Do you know, he's only got to point it in the right direction, and it will take him all the way home."

"He's not going home, Karli," Mutti said, taking Karli by the arm, and pulling him to his feet. "And I told you not to talk to him, didn't I?"

"It was my fault," the airman said, holding up his hands. "Look I am sorry…"

"You are always sorry," Mutti went on bitterly. "You are very good at being sorry. Well, you can be sorry in a prison camp. As soon as I can, I shall turn you over to the *Abwehr*, the police. They are bound to be out searching for you. They must have seen the parachute come down. Sooner or later they will come looking, and I shall turn you in. Meanwhile, you will not ingratiate yourself with my children. You will not speak to them, and they will not speak to you. Do you hear me? And if you try to run away, you will either freeze to death out there, or the *Abwehr* will catch you. Either way, you are not going home." She held out her hand for the compass. "And I will have that compass, please. Without it you are not going home, you are not going anywhere."

Peter took some time getting to his feet. He did not say a word. Towering over Mutti, he looked down at her, closed the compass and handed it to her.

2.

I REMEMBER STANDING THERE IN AUNT LOTTI'S kitchen watching this confrontation, and feeling very confused. I could not understand how Mutti could be like this. It seemed to me to be so hypocritical. All my life she had made herself out to be this ardent pacifist, always speaking out against the war – after all, there had been a huge rift in our family because of it – and now here she was full of unforgiving anger, and hateful, vengeful even, towards someone who may have been in the uniform of our enemy, but who was trying all he could to be kind and conciliatory and helpful. I wanted to tell her what I thought of her there and then, but I just did not feel

I could do so in front of Peter. It was not the moment.

And there was something else that was troubling me even more than this, something I was feeling and knew I should not be feeling, something I could not speak of, least of all to Mutti, and certainly not to Karli. I could tell no one because it was too terrible, because no one would understand. My mind was in turmoil. I had to get out. I ran out of the house, and went out across the farmyard to be with Marlene. It was as I was sitting there in the hay, watching her chomping away that I told her the dreadful truth that I dared tell no one else.

When I speak of it now, all these years later, I sound like a silly romantic girl, and of course, that is just what I was. I sat there, and I cried my heart out, and I told an elephant, an elephant if you please, that I loved this man – this airman, this enemy, whom I had not known even for twenty-four hours – that I knew I would love him till the day I died. It sounds ridiculous, I know, but that was how I felt, and when

you are sixteen you feel things very immediately, very strongly, very certainly.

"How wicked is that, Marlene?" I said. "How wicked is that, to love someone who should be my enemy, who has just bombed my city, killed my friends? How wicked is that?" I looked up into her weepy eye.

For an answer she wafted her ears gently at me, and groaned deep inside herself. It was enough to tell me that she had listened, and understood, and that she did not judge me. I learned something that day from Marlene, about friendship, and I have never forgotten it. To be a true friend, you have to be a good listener, and I discovered that day that Marlene was the truest of friends. For some time I stayed there out in Uncle Manfred's hay-barn. Marlene was the only being in the entire world that knew my secret, and I wanted to be with her and no one else. It was hard to bring myself to go back inside the house. I think it was only the cold that drove me back inside.

Exhausted, I suppose, from our long walk through the snow, and still trying to get ourselves warm, we were upstairs in bed by the late afternoon, all three of us in the big bedroom above the kitchen – Aunt Lotti and Uncle Manfred's room. We huddled there together under piles of blankets, leaving Peter downstairs sleeping in the chair by the stove. Mutti put a chair up against the bedroom door.

"I do not trust that man," she said, and I was far too tired to argue by then. We slept all through the rest of that day, and through the night.

When I came downstairs into the kitchen the next morning, Peter was sitting at the table, a map open in front of him. He smiled when he saw me, and called me over at once. "I want to show you something, Elizabeth. I have been thinking about this all night," he said. "You are travelling west, aren't you, away from the Russians? I have seen the roads, they are full of refugees, all going west. That is where I have to go too. So, you are going where I'm going. I think the nearest Allied armies are about

here, near Heidelberg. The American Army. They are about two hundred miles away, maybe more, I'm not sure. A long way, that's all I know. But with my compass, we could do it, I think. I cannot go by the roads – they will be too dangerous for me in my uniform. We could go across country, travel a lot by night, lie up by day. I have to go, I cannot just wait here to be caught. You understand?"

Mutti spoke up from behind me. I had not seen her come in. "We are going nowhere," she said icily.

"Then I shall have to go on my own," Peter told her. "I have to get home. Surely you can understand that?"

"So that you can come back to Germany and bomb us some more, I suppose," Mutti replied. She shrugged, and walked past him towards the stove. "You go if you want. I do not care any more. I cannot stop you, I know that now. It was foolish of me to think that I could. But we are staying here." She turned to me then. "Marlene will be needing some water, Elizabeth," she went on. "You could take her down to the stream. I noticed it was not iced up yesterday, it was still running…"

"All I was thinking… all I was trying to say," Peter interrupted, "was that I think we might all have a better chance if we stayed together, if we help one another. With my compass I can guide you to the Americans. And when we meet up with them, I could help."

"The children are too tired to move on," said Mutti. She was adamant. She would not hear of it. "And anyway, we do not need your help. We have managed quite well on our own up until now. We shall wait for a few days, for the snow to clear, and then move on. We do not need you, we do not want you."

I could no longer contain myself. I really gave her a piece of my mind. I told her she was just being ridiculous, that we did need Peter's help, and that she knew it. I stormed out then, went to the barn, and led Marlene down to the stream for a drink. She drank long and deep, enjoying every moment of it,

filling her trunk again and again and then pouring the water down her throat. Once she had finished drinking, she began sloshing her trunk about, and splashing me with icy water, which I did not appreciate at all. After a while I tried to encourage her to come away, leading her by the trunk, by the ear, imitating Karli's clicking noises, which I knew she responded to, trying to get her to move. But nothing I did or said would budge her from that stream. She wandered down into it now, ignoring me completely. I was wet, I told her, I was cold. I begged her to come out. But she was no longer in a listening mood. That was when I heard Mutti screaming, not from the house as I first thought it must be, but from the lakeside beyond.

I left Marlene and ran. I could hear Karli shrieking too now. It was not until I was through the farmyard gate and out into the field that I could begin to understand what was happening. There was a hole in the ice, about halfway between the lakeside and the island. It was Karli. He had fallen through the ice. All

I could see of him was a dark head, and flailing hands, as he struggled to grab a hold, as he tried to keep himself afloat. And Karli could not swim. Mutti was at the water's edge, screaming and crying, and Peter was there beside her, holding her back, his arms fast around her. She was fighting him, struggling to break free.

"You have to stay here," he was telling her. "Stay here. It's all right. I can reach him. Leave it to me."

Then he caught sight of me, and was shouting for me to go and fetch a rope.

I remembered that it was in the shed next to Tomi's stable that Uncle Manfred kept all his tools, all the harnesses, chains, ropes, everything. By the time I'd found a rope and run back with it down to the lakeside, I could see Peter was way out on the ice, down on his knees right by the hole, and reaching out for Karli who kept disappearing under the water.

Peter managed to grab hold of one of his hands and hang on. I tried to stop Mutti from going out on to the ice, but I wasn't strong enough. There was no way she would be left behind any longer. We clung to one another, hardly able to keep our balance, as we made our way gingerly across the ice towards them.

"That is far enough," Peter called. "Do not come any closer. Just hang on to one end of the rope, Elizabeth, and let me have the other."

I looped it quickly, whirled it around and around my head, and then threw it out as best I could, but the end of it fell short. I gathered it in, and tried again. This time it was close enough for Peter to reach out and catch hold of it. He was talking to Karli all the while, trying to calm him. Somehow he managed to get the rope around him, under his arms. "I've got him!" he cried. "Now pull, but pull gently."

As Mutti and I took the strain on the rope, we could see Peter had grabbed Karli by the back of his coat and was trying to haul him out. Moments later, Karli was lying there limp on the ice. Peter dragged

him away, then picked him up in his arms and came sliding and stumbling past us. Karli was grey in the face, and quite lifeless. Mutti was running alongside them, calling all the while for Karli to wake up.

Once inside the house, Peter laid Karli down in front of the stove, and, with Mutti, peeled off his wet clothes, rubbed him down vigorously and covered him with blankets. All I could do was stand there and watch, desperate for any sign of life in my little brother. There was none, no movement, no breathing. Mutti was beside herself with despair by now, weeping over Karli and trying to shake him awake. Peter helped her to her feet and turned to me.

"Look after your mother, will you?" he said. So I put my arms around her, and just held her tight. All we could do was look on in horror and in hope, as Peter knelt over Karli, hands flat on Karli's chest, pumping him, then lifting his chin and blowing deep into his mouth, then pumping again and again. Long minutes went by, the longest of my life, and still Karli did not respond. His lips were blue, and there was a stillness about him that I knew could only mean that it was over, that there was no point in going on, that nothing could be done now to bring him back to life.

But Peter was not giving up on him, not for one moment. He stopped only to put his ear to Karli's chest to listen for his breathing. "Come on, Karli!" he shouted. "Come on!" And then on he went, pumping, pumping.

I turned to Mutti and buried my head in her shoulder, both of us weeping uncontrollably. That was when we both heard the sound of spluttering. I looked, and saw Karli's eyes opening, and then he was coughing and choking, the water was spurting up out of his mouth on to the kitchen floor. It kept coming and coming, until at last it was all out and he lay there breathing hard, a great smile coming over his face as he recognised us.

Peter sat back on his haunches, his hands over his face. I wanted to hug him there and then, hug him tight and never let him go. Mutti was on her knees, cradling Karli in her arms and kissing him all over his face, and

Karli was strong enough already to try to push her away – he was never that fond of being kissed, by Mutti, or by me, or by anyone else, come to that. I knelt down in front of Peter then, and took his hands away from his face. I could see he had been crying too. I knew then in that moment as our eyes met, that he felt for me what I was feeling for him.

"Thank you," I said, still holding his hands in mine. "Thank you, thank you." At the time, I think this was almost all the English I knew. Tears soon gave way to laughter though as Mutti berated Karli. She was back to being an exasperated mother.

"Why? What were you doing out there on the ice, Karli?" she cried. "What were you thinking of?"

"I was only trying to get to the island," Karli said, "to see the tree house Papi built for us. I was nearly there, and then the ice broke. It was not my fault. It was the ice's fault. It was too thin."

Uncle Manfred's clothes were a little on the small side for Peter, we discovered, and the trousers hung loose around his waist, but they were dry, and that was all that mattered. He was soon sitting by the stove, with Karli still wrapped up in a blanket beside him, and Karli was telling him all about our tree house on the island, and how the two of us used to play pirates over there, pirates from *Treasure Island* – Papi's favourite book when he was a boy – and how Karli was always Long John Silver because he was better at limping than I was, and because he was better at being bloodthirsty than I was too.

All this time Mutti was at the stove busying herself making potato soup. She had gone quite silent, I noticed. She seemed deep in thought. She had not said a word to Peter since Karli's rescue, not even when he came downstairs dressed in Uncle Manfred's clothes and clogs. Karli and I had laughed and laughed, but Mutti still looked stony-faced. There was a change though. She was no longer telling us not to speak to him, and the pitchfork was nowhere to be seen. We were sitting down at the table, enjoying the warmth of our soup, and Karli was still playing at being Long John Silver. It was "Yo ho ho!" after every

sip of soup, accompanied by his squawky parrot noises.

Peter and I looked at one another over our soup, and smiled. We were not only smiling at Karli's antics, we were smiling into each other's eyes.

I knew at once that it was the police at the door, the moment I heard the knocking. I saw the alarm in Peter's eyes. No one knocks on a door like the police.

3.

"MAY WE COME IN?"

It wasn't a request. It was a demand. There were three of them, and they were soldiers, not policemen. With their rifles, helmets and greatcoats they seemed to fill the room.

"You live here?" the soldier asked. One of them did the talking, while the others walked around the room as if they were searching for something, or someone.

"My sister does," Mutti said, "with her husband. But they have gone away. We're living here now, me, my daughter and my two sons. My husband is away fighting the Russians."

"We are looking for a parachutist. There were reports of a parachute coming down not far from here. An enemy bomber was shot down, a Lancaster. British. It crashed only a few kilometres away. We found the wreckage. One of the bastards is here somewhere. So we are searching every house, every farm. Have you seen anyone?"

"No one," Mutti replied. "We are alone here. We only came yesterday, from Dresden. We escaped from the city."

"There is no city any more," said the policeman. "There is no Dresden. There are so many dead. It is impossible to know how many. Bastards. Bastards. I tell you if we find this one, a prison camp is too good for him. We will shoot him first and ask questions later."

Someone was shouting from outside. "Sergeant, Sergeant! You must come, come quickly!" Another soldier, this one much younger, appeared at the door, breathless with excitement. "You are not going to believe this, Sergeant. But there is an elephant, out there, in the barn."

"An elephant?"

"Yes, Sergeant. We were searching the outbuildings like you said, and we went into the barn, and there he was."

"She is a she," said Mutti. "She is called Marlene. I work in the zoo, with the elephants, in Dresden. She was the only animal we managed to save. The rest had to be shot because of the bombing. I have brought her here to the family farm. I knew of nowhere else to go."

The youngest of the soldiers was told to stay with us and guard us, while the others went out. Karli was about to say something, but Mutti frowned at him quickly and put a finger to her lips. The clock on the wall ticked loudly in the silence. I could not bear the tension. I felt for Peter's hand under the table, and found it. We heard them coming back across the yard, their voices loud with excitement. Then they were back in the kitchen.

"This elephant, she is not dangerous?" the Sergeant asked.

Mutti shook her head. "I will look after her," she told them. "I have known this elephant ever since she was born. She is as gentle as a kitten, I promise you."

"And you have seen no airman, no parachutist?" he went on.

"No," Mutti said. She spoke very coolly. "If I saw one, after all they have done in Dresden, I would shoot him myself."

"Your papers?" he demanded. "I want to see your papers."

"I'm sorry. We haven't got them. They are all in Dresden, in our house," said Mutti, shrugging her shoulders. "We were outside, out in the park, when we heard the air-raid sirens, and then the bombers. We just ran."

"Names then," said the sergeant, taking out his notebook. "I must have your names."

Mutti gave our names, all of us, Peter's last of all.

"And how old are you?" the Sergeant asked Peter. I sensed suspicion in his look. I could hear it in his voice.

"Twenty-one," Peter told him.

"So why are you not in uniform, in the army?"

Peter hesitated. It was Karli who spoke up for him. "He gets asthma like me," he said. "When he gets puffed out he gets asthma. Everyone at school says that when I grow up, I can't be a soldier, and I want to be a—"

"That's right," Mutti interrupted. "My son has been excused military service, on medical grounds – asthma."

I was not at all sure the sergeant believed what he was hearing. I felt certain that there would be more questions. But, amazingly, there were not.

When the sergeant saluted, I remember Karli gave him the *Hitlergruss,* the stiff arm Hitler salute we had all been taught at school, and said "Heil Hitler," with great enthusiasm and conviction. He was playing his part perfectly. And then the soldiers were gone. I could feel my heart pounding in my neck as I listened to the last of their voices and their laughter drifting away outside. All they were chatting about as they left was the elephant in the barn, and the zoo in Dresden. One of them had been for a ride on an elephant in that zoo when he was little, he was saying. And then nothing more.

Mutti went to the window to make sure. "It is all right, they have gone," she whispered.

She came over and sat down at the table with us, her face drained of all colour. For several moments Peter and Mutti did not speak, but sat there just looking at one another across the kitchen.

Mutti took a long breath and said, "You didn't finish your soup, Peter. It will be getting cold. Eat, eat." Then she fished in her pocket, took out the compass, and pushed it across the table towards him. "Yours, I think."

"Thank you," Peter said, as he took it. "And for what you did just then, thank you."

"You and I, Peter, we must come to an understanding," Mutti went on. "From now on, no more 'sorry's, and no more 'thank you's. What is done is done. The past is behind us. You are family now, one of us. And I have been thinking. You were right when you told Elizabeth we should stick together and help one another. We do all want to go west, away from the Russians, away from the bombing. So we shall go together, and across country, as you said. It will be safer for all of us. Can that compass thing really guide us to the Americans?"

Peter smiled. "Yes, all the way, if we can keep going, if we get lucky. But I have been thinking too, and I am not so sure now that it is such a good idea to stick together. I was not thinking straight when I said it. If they discover who I am… I mean, we got away with it once, we may not be so lucky next time. They will shoot you if they ever find out who I am. You do know that, don't you?"

"Who is going to tell them?" Mutti replied. "I'm not going to tell them, am I? Nor will Elizabeth, nor will Karli. Like I said, we are family. You speak good German, and you even look quite German in Uncle Manfred's clothes. We fooled them once, with a little help from Karli, didn't we? We can fool them again."

"Maybe you are right. I hope so. But – and I did not want to have to say this – I think there is another problem. The elephant, your Marlene." I could see Peter was reluctant to go on. "Listen, if we take her with us, we are bound to attract attention to ourselves. It will be more dangerous. I think we should leave her here. There is plenty of hay in the barn, we could fill up buckets of water…"

"Where we go Marlene goes," Mutti said firmly. "She is part of the family too. What does it say in that book – *The Three Musketeers*, wasn't it? – 'All for one and one for all'."

I remember Mutti made us all join hands round the table then, for another 'family moment', as we had so often done back home. Even Karli knew better than to interrupt this family ritual. Maybe he was praying as hard as I was. I was praying for Papi to come home, for us all to find the Americans, for us all to survive – and for Peter to go on holding my hand as tight as he was, and never let go. But in the end it was Karli, of course, who eventually decided this family moment had gone on quite long enough, and broke the silence.

"When are we going?" he asked. "How far is it? I want to ride up on Marlene all the way. I can, can't I, Mutti? How long will it take until we get there?"

We spent all the rest of that day poring over Peter's map, making plans, working out how far we could hope to travel each night. Peter thought we could do about eight to ten kilometres a night, depending on the weather, and if we kept up that pace, and the Americans kept advancing at their present rate, then he calculated we had a good chance of meeting up with them in four or five weeks or so. We packed up all the food we could find, all we could carry, and put on all the warm clothes we needed. We all had full rucksacks, and a rolled-up blanket strapped on top of

each of them. We had a last meal, the rest of the potato soup, and some cheese, left a note, which we all signed, to Uncle Manfred and Aunt Lotti, thanking them, and telling them where we were going.

Then we stepped out into the moonlit farmyard to fetch Marlene from the barn, the snow crisp and crunching under our feet. Marlene had to be enticed away from her hay – and that was not easy – but Karli managed it with a few tempting potatoes. Then once outside the barn, Peter hoisted Karli up on to her back, and we set off into the night, westwards, Mutti leading Marlene by the ear, Karli clicking at Marlene all the while, telling her to gee up. Peter and I walked on ahead together, Peter with compass in hand. We were on our way."

Part Four

Ring of Bells

l.

LIZZIE PAUSED FOR A FEW MOMENTS THEN, AND RAISED HER hand. "Listen," she said, gazing out of the window. "Bells, do you hear them?" I hadn't, not until that moment. "I love the sound of church bells ringing," she went on. "Every time I hear a ring of bells, it makes me think the same thing, that there is hope, that life goes on. Did you know that in Dresden every year on the anniversary of the day the bombers came, they ring all the church bells in the city? I have been back a few times now. It is not the old city, of course, but it is wonderful to see how they have built it up again, out of the ashes; and when the bells ring out over the new city, they are a lot louder than this one, I promise you. But this one is beautiful. This is a gentle bell."

She turned to us then. "I am sorry my story has taken so long. It is getting dark outside already. I do go on, I know. Maybe you were right after all, maybe I should tell you the rest another day. It is good of you to have listened this long."

"Listening, it's what friends are for, remember?" I said.

"Did you escape?" Karl asked. "Did Peter get caught? What happened? I want to know what happened."

"You see?" I said, with a smile." We're not going anywhere till you tell us the rest of the story. We're staying right where we are, aren't we, Karl?"

Lizzie patted my hand. "You are both very kind," she said. "I will not keep you long now, I promise." She stroked the glass face of the compass with the tips of her fingers, contemplated it for a while, and then went on with her story.

"Without this compass, and without Peter, I think we would never have made it. He was so right to keep us away from the roads. We were to learn that it was not the cold and the hunger that were the greatest threat to us, it was people, people who might be suspicious of us, who would ask questions, who would report us. Out in the countryside there were not many people. And if we had joined the thousands of people cramming the roads there would have been even greater dangers to face – the planes, the fighters. They told us all about it, some of the refugees we came across later, how the planes would come flying in low over the roads, bombing and strafing.

So many died that way, soldiers and refugees, side by side.

Peter and his compass kept us away from all that.

But I am sure it was also because we travelled always by night that we survived. I remember, Mutti was for ever worrying that we were moving

too slowly, that the Russians were closing in behind us. It was true that we could often hear the distant rumble of their guns. We saw them lighting up the night sky all along the eastern horizon, and they did seem to be coming much closer all the time. After trekking through the night, Mutti must have been as exhausted as we all were, but she was reluctant to stop each

morning. She always felt we could keep going a little while longer.

Thankfully, by the first glimmer of every dawn Peter had usually managed to find somewhere for us to hide up for the day, somewhere we could at least be dry and warm, and even light a fire if we were lucky. It might be some remote barn, or shepherd's hut or forester's shack — it didn't matter. All the time we stayed away from any towns and villages, and kept as far as possible to the valleys and woods where we would be less likely to be seen. We soon discovered we were not the only ones tramping through the countryside on that long trek westwards, nor the only ones who had chosen to avoid the dangers of the roads.

So there were days, like it or not, when we would find ourselves having to share a barn or shed with other refugees, mostly families like us. But once or twice there were soldiers with us too, whole units of them. Those meetings were awkward at first. No one trusted anyone in those days, you see. You never could, not to begin with. It was having Marlene with us that helped break the ice, helped dispel suspicion. They would only have to see Marlene, and Mutti would only have to tell our story about the zoo, and how we had looked after Marlene at home in the garden, and soon they would be telling their own stories, of how they had escaped the bombing and the

firestorm. All of us knew we were lucky to be alive. Strange to say, considering what we were all living through, there was often more laughter than tears, though I do remember there were many refugees who just sat there staring into nothing, rocking back and forth, and murmuring in their misery.

If there were other children there, then Karli loved it all the more. Not only did he have an audience for his juggling and all his party tricks, but he had Marlene to show off with as well. Somehow he had taught Marlene to kneel down and to lift her trunk at his command, and the children loved this. In front of them he always claimed absolute ownership of Marlene. He referred to her as 'my elephant' or 'my Marlene'. He just loved play-acting, and he was good at it too.

He had slipped easily into the part of being a younger brother to Peter — mostly, I think, because he genuinely liked having an older brother of his own, a proper pal. He would tell everyone proudly that he was the only one that could handle the elephant, that his older brother could not manage her at all, and certainly not his sister. He played the clown wonderfully, and people laughed. I found that once we had laughed together for a while, we all began to feel there was a kind of refugee solidarity amongst us, a camaraderie, sometimes so much so that we did not just swap stories, but food and drink as well.

But on Mutti's advice, Peter kept himself to himself, and did not talk too much when there were other people about, and that was just as well. The more we got to know him, the more we noticed that he did have a noticeable accent. Canadian or Swiss, it did not matter. All that mattered was that he spoke differently enough for other people to notice it, and if we noticed it, then they might too.

Time and again people would ask Mutti why her son was not in uniform like all the other young men. Mutti stuck always to the asthma

story Karli had first made up in front of the policeman that day. It was a good cover story because, of course, she knew all the symptoms rather well. We all did, except for Peter himself that is, but at Mutti's suggestion, Karli had made sure that Peter knew exactly what it felt like to suffer from asthma. He even taught Peter how to cough and wheeze the right way. Nonetheless, it still made me very nervous every time the subject came up. I was fearful too because, after living through the horror of the bombing of Dresden, everyone we came across was full of anger and bitterness against the Americans and the British. Until now, much of this hatred had been reserved more for the Russians. Not now, not any more. So Peter, if he were to be discovered, would be in real danger. And so would we.

Most of the other refugees we met were from Dresden, like us, though a few had come from further east. For them in particular, fear of the Russians still far outweighed any anger against the

Americans and the British. There were many stories of dreadful atrocities committed by the Red Army on civilians as they advanced deeper and deeper into Germany. I did not know then, and I do not know now, what was true and what was not, but I do know that many of our fellow refugees were terrified of the Russians. I only know that there is always atrocity in war. We heard too that the Red Army was closer now than we had thought, only a few miles the other side of Dresden. So despite all the Allied bombing, everyone thought it was better to be at the mercy of the Americans and the British, rather than to wait for the Russians to arrive.

Whenever we found ourselves hiding away in the company of other refugees, Peter would make himself scarce, to avoid suspicious looks and searching questions, he told me. Sometimes he said he was off to look for food, but often he would excuse himself by saying that he had to see to Marlene. And whenever I could, I would go

with him, not of course to help with Marlene at all, but just because I wanted to be with him. We wanted to be together now all we could, and alone too. The two of us would spend long hours sitting there beside Marlene, out in some barn or shed, as she munched her hay or straw – whatever we had found for her. Or we would be watching her from a river bank, drinking and sluicing herself down.

It was during these times together that Peter began to tell me about his home in Canada, in Toronto, of the parts he had played in the theatre, mostly walk-on parts: a spear-carrier, a servant, a policeman, a butler. He would tell me about the cabin deep in the forest – he called it his 'cottage' – where he and his mother and father used to go for weekends all through his childhood, about the cycling and the canoeing they did, and the salmon fishing, and the moose and the black bears they saw. And I told him about Papi, about Uncle Manfred and Aunt Lotti, and all the good times we had had down on the farm, and about the argument that had split the family.

But we tried all we could not to talk about the war. We both of us knew it was the grim shadow that hung over us, that threatened to separate us, and we both wanted to live for a while away from all of that, in the warm sunlight of shared memories and hopes. We found we had so much in common - bicycling, boating and fishing. He was an only child, he told me, and had never been part of a large family, until now, that is. He knew he was only playing the part of the elder brother, but the longer he was with us the more he felt easy in the part, just one of the family, and he loved that, he said.

How we talked, but even in our silences I felt a togetherness with him that I had never felt with anyone else.

Then came the time – well, I suppose it had to happen, didn't it? – that Karli came upon us one day and surprised us. I remember we were sitting there on the river bank, with Marlene

wafting her trunk over our heads.

"You two, you are canoodling, aren't you?" he said, with a mischievous twinkle in his eye. "I know you are. You are always going off together. I have been watching you."

"None of your business," I snapped. I was furious with him and embarrassed too. But Peter handled it much better. He sat him down between us and put his arm around him.

"We were just talking, Karli, getting to know one another. I am her brother, remember? Your brother too. You and me, we talk, don't we? The thing is, that if I want to play a part right, I have to get right into it. That is why you told me all about your asthma attacks, remember? I need to know all there is to know about the new me, and my new family. I have to know the back-stories of everyone in the play. See what I'm saying? It is what actors do. You understand that, don't you, Karli? I mean, people might ask me questions, about Papi, for instance, about where we lived in

Dresden, about the zoo, about the farm, about Uncle Manfred and Aunt Lotti. I've got to know these things, right? Elizabeth, she is just telling me all she can, to help me."

Karli seemed happy enough with that, but there were many times after that when I could feel he was keeping an eye on us, and that worried me. I certainly did not want Mutti to have any idea how I really felt about Peter. Not because of what she might think about it, but because it was private, very personal, and I wanted to keep it that way.

The food we had brought with us from the farm lasted as long as we could make it, but in the end of course there was none left. After that, finding something to eat became our greatest problem. Not for Marlene. She would only have to brush the snow aside with her trunk or her foot, to be able to find something edible underneath. And once the snow had gone, Marlene simply grazed as she went. She was on a

constant scrounge, her trunk searching ahead of her. For much of our journey we kept to the valleys, so there was always plenty of water for us to drink, from the rivers and streams. And there were many days when Peter found us a hay-barn to hide in where Marlene could gorge herself all day long.

But food for us was much harder to find. Again, it was Peter who saved our bacon, so to speak. In the air force he had done some training in living off the land – it was something they all had to do, in case they got shot down. And anyway, luckily for us, back home in Canada he was used to finding food in the wild, scavenging for it, fishing for it, hunting for it. He had done this all his life, but, as he said, until now scavenging had not included stealing.

Early every morning we would settle into our new shelter for the day, make ourselves and Marlene as comfortable as we could, and then sooner or later Peter would disappear. He would

be back an hour or so later with something: eggs
from a hen-house maybe, or a sausage, 'liberated'
he called it, from someone's larder. There were
carrots sometimes, even apples once or twice. It
turned out that there were many homes and farms
lying empty and deserted in the countryside. So
many people, like Uncle Manfred and Aunt Lotti,
had abandoned their houses and fled.

And Peter scavenged for more than food.
Once he came back with a fishing rod, and after
that we quite often had grilled fish for our

breakfast. But there were
times when he came back
with very little: a few nuts
and some half-rotten
root vegetables. Several
times he returned empty-
handed altogether. Then
we just went hungry,
and those were the
days, with no food

inside us, when it was hardest to keep ourselves warm, even if we could manage to make a fire.

Those were the worst times during our whole long trek, the days of hunger. The endless walking I got used to. I even got used to my blisters, to my freezing hands and ears, and my numb feet. The snow went away, but the cold never did. Sometimes, when I felt I could not take another step, I would feel Mutti's arm around me, and she would say always the same thing, "Just put one foot in front of the other, Elizabeth, and we'll get there." It was her constant mantra. When I was at my lowest ebb, I would keep saying that to myself, trying my very hardest to believe it. There were so many times when I came close to giving up altogether.

Thinking back, though, it was Marlene as much as Mutti's mantra that kept me going. Through wind and rain, mud and frost, Marlene just plodded on. She was our pace-maker, and we kept with her. When I was walking anywhere near her I could hear the hollow rumblings of contentment from inside her. And that for some reason always made me smile, and so lifted my spirits. We all envied her ability to find food on the move, snuffling up dead leaves, tugging at what little grass there was. We took great comfort and courage from her endless patience and perseverance. And she treated us all now, Peter included, with great affection, as if we were her family. We certainly felt she was part of ours. She was for ever touching us with the soft tip of her trunk, reassuring us, and reassuring herself maybe. If Peter was our guide and provider, and Mutti was our strength, then Marlene was our inspiration.

Sometimes, after the long hours of walking through the darkness of the countryside, when we were all hungry and cold and tired, and the night seemed never-ending, Mutti would get us singing. We would sing her beloved Marlene Dietrich songs, or Christmas carols, or the nursery

rhymes and folk songs Karli and I had grown up with. Peter knew some of these from his Swiss mother, so he would join in then too. Of course Karli would sing out louder than any of us, conducting everyone from high up on Marlene. These were the moments, as we were singing our way through the night, that I felt all my fears fly away. I felt suddenly light-headed, and full of hope, hope that all would be well. I cannot imagine why just singing together should be able to do this, but it did. It did not only pass the time. Somehow it lifted my heart, gave me new strength, and fresh determination just to keep going. It was the same for all of us, I think.

I suppose we must have been three weeks or so into our journey across Germany, and we were making much slower progress than Peter had expected. It was the streams and rivers that were holding us up. Streams we could have forded easily enough – Marlene seemed quite happy to go back and forth carrying two of us at a time.

But to cross the rivers we had to find a bridge, and a bridge that was not guarded, as many of them were. So whenever we came to a bridge, Peter had to scout ahead to find out if there were sentries. And if there were, it meant a long diversion along the river until we found an unguarded bridge. This made our journey a lot longer, and so we lost a lot of time that way.

We knew that anyone and everyone who saw us or met up with us was a danger to us, but we could not avoid them altogether, however hard we tried. Even at night we did meet a few people, some walking home to their village after dark, or sometimes shepherds out in their fields checking their sheep; and once a farmer, I remember, who we came upon suddenly behind a hedge. He was trying to help one of his cows give birth, and he needed a hand, he said. So Peter got down on his knees at once, and pulled alongside the farmer. It took a while, but the calf came out alive and kicking. The farmer was delighted, and shook all

our hands energetically. It was only after it was all over that he seemed to pay any attention to Marlene. Mutti told him our story, and he seemed quite happy with that. We had a night in his barn and his wife brought us some hot soup. They asked no questions, but kept bringing more and more of their family in to see Marlene. Far from attracting unwelcome attention to us, as Peter had thought, Marlene was turning out to be a kind of talisman. She seemed to divert attention away from us, and away from Peter in particular, which was of course just what we wanted.

Hidden away during the daytime, huddled together inside some shed or barn, we had heard and sometimes seen fighter planes flying low overhead, but we were safe from them, always well out of sight. Day and night we had heard too the drone of bombers overhead, but like the fighters, they passed us by, and left us in peace. Had it not been for the ever more distant thunder of Russian guns we might almost have been able to forget that there was a war going on at all. The deeper we went into the countryside, the quieter it became and the safer we felt. There were some days and nights so still and silent now, that it really seemed to me sometimes as if the war might have ended already, and we just had not heard about it.

I remember Karli became ill quite quickly. Weakened by his asthma, he had never been a

strong child. It began one evening with a little cough that would not leave him. Mutti swathed him in blankets, and for the best part of that night he rode up on Marlene as usual, but it was becoming obvious after a while that he just did not have the strength to stay up there, that he could fall off at any time. Much against his will Mutti persuaded him down, and carried him the rest of the way in her arms.

Peter and I were scouting ahead, looking urgently now for a place to shelter — anywhere would do, just so long as we could get Karli out of the cold. There were no lights in the houses, of course, because of the black-out. But it was a moonlit night, which was why I caught sight of the dark looming shape of a huge building in the distance, and then the ribbon of a tree-lined drive curving through the fields towards it. From the sound of his cough and his wheezing, we could tell that Karli was getting worse all the time. He needed more than just a shelter for the night, he needed a doctor. We had no choice. We knew it was a risk, but we walked straight up the gravel drive and knocked loudly on the huge front door. It was a while before anyone came, and Peter was beginning to think that the house had been abandoned like so many others. But then the door opened. We saw the light of a lantern. Holding it was an old man in pyjamas and nightcap.

He did not look at all friendly.

2.

"IT IS THE MIDDLE OF THE NIGHT," GROWLED THE OLD man. "What is it that you want?"

"Please. We need a doctor," Mutti told him. "My son, he is very sick. Please."

Then from further inside the house came another voice, a woman's voice. "Who is it, Hans? Is it more of them? Let them in."

The door opened wider, and we saw then a lady in a dressing gown, coming down a huge wide staircase, and then hurrying towards us across the hallway.

"She says they need a doctor, Countess," the old man said. They were both peering at us now, from behind the lamplight.

"We are from Dresden," Mutti told them.

"Am I seeing things?" the lady asked. "Or is that an elephant?"

"I can explain about that later," Mutti replied. "But my son is ill, seriously ill, and I have to find a doctor. Please. It is urgent."

The lady did not hesitate. She took Mutti by the arm and led her into the hallway. "Come in, come in," she said. "I shall send for the doctor from the village

right away. And Hans, you will find a place for that animal in the stables."

I had no idea that night who these people were, and neither did I care. We would soon have a doctor for Karli, and we had found shelter for him too. That was all that mattered. And it would be warm too. I could even smell food. But I did not get to go in right away. Mutti asked me to take care of Marlene, and to make sure that she had something to eat and drink. So, led by Hans, the old man in the nightcap, who muttered angrily to himself the whole time, I took her round the side of the house, through a great archway and into a stable yard. I saw to it that she had all she needed, hay and water both, and left her to it. She seemed quite happy, happier certainly than the horses across the yard from her, who were becoming increasingly unsettled at the appearance of this strange intruder.

As we walked back towards the house – the place seemed immense to me, more like a castle than a house – Hans was still grumbling on, but less to himself and rather more to me, about how he could never get a good night's sleep any more, how it was bad enough that the countess had opened her doors to all and sundry, but now she was turning the stable yard into a zoo. It was all too much, he said, too much.

It was not until he was leading me back into the house and up the grand staircase that I began to see for myself what he was complaining about. Everywhere I looked, every centimetre of floor space, was occupied. People were lying fast asleep, in the corridors, on the landings, and, I presumed, in every room. And those that were not asleep were sitting there on straw-filled sacks looking up at me blankly as I passed by. There was bewilderment on every face I saw. Hans took me up to the top of the house, to the attic, where I saw Karli lying stretched out on a mattress by a fire with Mutti kneeling over him, bathing his forehead. Peter was busy piling more wood on the fire.

"He has a fever, Elizabeth," Mutti said, looking up at me, her eyes full of tears. "He's burning up. Where

is that doctor? Where is he?"

For the rest of that night Karli lay there tossing and turning, sometimes delirious, and all three of us took it in turns to try to cool him. None of us slept, we just sat there watching him, hoping the fever would leave him, longing for the doctor to come. When he did come at long last, the lady came with him, dressed now rather grandly, and all in black. The doctor examined him, and said that Karli should be kept warm at all costs, and that the more water we could get him to drink the better. The doctor gave us some medicine for Karli and told us that on no account was he to go out in the cold, or travel, until he was completely well again.

It was only now, once he had gone, that the lady in black introduced herself. "Everyone just calls me Countess," she said, shaking each of us rather formally by the hand. "We do not bother much with names here – it is safer that way. I think we have about seventy refugees now in the house – all sorts, mostly families from the east resting up for a few days. Everyone is passing through. It seems as if the whole world is in flight. We have soldiers on their way home on leave, or returning to their regiments at the front, some deserters no doubt, and we have a few vagrants too. I ask no questions. We have a hot meal only once a day, at midday, and then soup and bread in the evening. It is not much, but it is the best we can manage, I'm afraid. As you know, food is becoming very scarce everywhere now. You may stay as long as you like, certainly until the young boy is better, but I would not advise you to stay on much longer after that. The Russians are not so far away now, maybe a few weeks away, no more. The Americans are closer, by all accounts, but who knows who will get here first?"

Mutti thanked her from the bottom of her heart for all her kindness towards us.

"Having said I ask no questions," the Countess went on, with a smile, "I have to say that I am rather curious about the elephant."

As Mutti told her the story about working in the zoo, about Papi being away fighting in Russia, and

about our escape with Marlene from Dresden, the Countess listened intently.

Then she said, "I too had a husband in the army once, but he is dead now. And like you I also have a son. Like your husband, he is fighting the Russians in the east. Maybe they know one another, you never know." She was looking very directly at Peter now. "My son is just about your age, I think," she said. "And he has brown eyes, deep-set like yours. It is my greatest wish to see him again, alive and well. We can only hope."

We stayed on with the countess for several days. It took Karli three or four of those days to recover. Peter gave him the compass to look after, and that made Karli so happy. He would go to sleep clutching it in his fist. I remember he told Peter once, that it was better than any teddy bear. And he said afterwards, when he was well again, that he was sure it was Peter's compass that had made him better in the end, and not the doctor's medicine.

Mutti did not want to risk setting out again on our travels until she was quite sure Karli was strong enough.

The trouble was that the longer we stayed and the more comfortable we became, the more we did not want to leave. We would sit down at midday with all the other refugees in the great dining hall and eat good hot food. It was the countess who was responsible for creating a feeling of great fellowship amongst us. She made us all so welcome. She took time and trouble with everyone. She was generous too, and thoughtful. When Karli told her he was good at juggling one day, she gave him two tennis balls – if he was happy, it would help him to get better, she said.

As the countess had told us, all sorts of people were there, coming and going, and everyone had a story to tell – and as it turned out, a song to sing as well. There was a group of twenty or so school children that arrived just a day or so after we did. These were the children we got to know best, and of course that was because of Marlene, and Karli too. Once Karli told them – and naturally he wasted no time in doing this – that we had had an elephant living in the garden back home, that we had brought

her with us, that she was living out in the stable yard right now, we could not keep them away.

With Karli getting stronger every day now, it was impossible to keep him inside for long. Mutti tried to make him stay on his mattress up in the attic, but he was for ever going missing. We always knew where to find him of course. He would be down there with Marlene, both of them surrounded by a large audience of admirers. The school children were utterly amazed by the elephant, and they loved to watch Karli doing his juggling tricks too. But what they loved best of all, was when Karli decided he would perform his juggling act high up there astride Marlene's neck! And that was how Karli, quite unintentionally, landed us all in very great danger.

One afternoon, I came into the stable yard with Peter and Mutti, looking for Karli, who had disappeared, yet again. We saw him sitting up there on Marlene, and juggling away. There was a whole crowd around him – Hans, the countess's manservant, was there, and forty, maybe fifty of our fellow refugees, and the school children – and Karli was showing off even

more than usual. As he juggled, he was telling everyone about how he had ridden Marlene all the way from Dresden. I shall never know what made him do it. But suddenly he just stopped his juggling, plunged his hand into his pocket, and held up the compass. "You know what this is?" he said proudly. "This is my big brother Peter's magic compass. He just follows where the arrow points, and we follow him. It is how we got here. Simple."

"Juggle with it!" one of the school children called out. "I bet you cannot do it with three!" Then they were all clamouring for him to dare to do it. "Go on, Karli! Go on!"

I shouted at him not to, but I knew even then that it was no use, that he would be unable to resist the temptation to show off even more. I pushed my way through the crowd to try to stop him, but I was too late. He was already juggling by the time I got there, with the two balls and the compass.

For a while it looked fine. He was juggling brilliantly. I had seen him juggling as many as four balls before, many a time, and he had hardly ever dropped one. I am sure it was because of all the hullabaloo the crowd were making that Marlene was becoming a little unsettled. She was wafting her ears, and swaying from side to side, a sure sign she was agitated. Then she lifted her trunk and shifted forward suddenly, throwing Karli off balance. I saw the compass flying high into the air. I dashed forward to try to catch it. I think I knew it was hopeless, that it was way out of my reach, that there was no way I could make it. I tripped then and fell heavily.

When I looked up I saw that Hans had caught the compass and was holding it in his cupped hands. I was just relieved it was not broken. The children were all clapping and cheering. I had noticed before that Hans never smiled. And he was not smiling now either, despite all the applause. He was turning the compass over in his hands, examining it carefully. He flicked it open, and then looked up at Karli.

"Where did you get this?" he demanded. "It is not German. This looks to me like a British compass, or

American. A German compass would have O for *Ost*, and this has an E. *Ost* in English is East. And there is English writing on it too. Where did you get it?"

A sudden silence had descended on the stable yard. Karli for once had nothing to say. His eyes met mine. He was begging for help. But I couldn't think of anything to say either.

"I asked you where you got it from?" Hans said again.

"From me." It was Mutti's voice from behind me. She had Peter with her as she came through the crowd towards me. She put her arm around my shoulder. "My husband gave it to me. A gift. He is fighting the Russians now, but at the beginning of the war he was in France, in Normandy. He told me he got it off a British pilot who had been shot down. It was his, and now it is mine," she said. I admired her so much at that moment. I knew she was brave, but had no idea she could be this inventive.

Hans hesitated for a long time. I could see he had his doubts, that he still was not sure he believed her.

"Thank you," Mutti went on, "for catching it, I mean. I would hate to have seen it lying there smashed on the ground. It was the last gift I had from my husband. It has brought us all the way from Dresden, you know. So, for lots of reasons, you can see it is very precious to me, to my whole family. Thank you."

Hans seemed more satisfied now. He thought for a while, then nodded slowly, before handing it over to her at last. "It is not a toy," he said. "I do not think little children should be playing with such a thing."

"I quite agree," Mutti replied, with a shrug and a smile. "But you know how children are. Don't you worry. I will see to it that he does not do it again, I promise you."

She looked up at Karli. She did not have to pretend to be angry with him. Karli knew it. He was looking quite shamefaced and sheepish.

"Karli, you will get down off that elephant this minute, and come with me."

Peter went to help him down, and once we had seen Marlene safely back in her stable, we all walked away. But I could feel Hans's eyes on us all the time.

After supper that same evening the countess got up and clapped her hands to quieten everyone down. "What many of you do not know," she began, "is that the school children we have with us are from a chapel choir in Dresden. I have asked them if they would sing something for us. In these terrible times I think it is only music that can bring us some joy and peace of mind. Only last Christmas, they told me, they sang 'The Christmas Oratorio' by Johann Sebastian Bach, who is for me the greatest German who ever lived. They have very kindly agreed to sing some of it for us now."

As they were singing, I found I could lose myself completely in the music, that I could forget all the dreadful things that were going on in the world. I felt cocooned in this heavenly music. It seemed to warm me all through. It was a glow that lingered long after the singing had finished. I was still hearing it again in my head when we were back upstairs in our attic room that night, huddled under our blankets. The music had affected us all just as deeply, I think. We could talk about nothing else. Even Mutti had stopped being angry with Karli about the compass incident.

"I only wish Papi could have been there with us to hear his beloved Bach," she said. "He would have loved it so much."

We were almost asleep when the door opened, and the light of a lantern danced into the room. It was the countess. She crouched down to speak to us, talking in a hushed voice.

"I am afraid there is trouble," she said. "Hans is a good man. He has been with me for over forty years now. He was in the last war and is a loyal German, as I

am. But he and I, we have different loyalties, different ideas. I have learned that he intends to go to the police, about the compass – yes, he has told me everything that happened. I tried to persuade him not to, but he insisted that it was his patriotic duty. I am afraid he did not believe your story, and I have to say, neither do I. But I have another reason to doubt you. Your son." She was looking directly at Peter now. "How you speak, this has been troubling me for quite a while now. When you talk, you sound to me like an American. You see, I have relatives in America, and when they speak German, they speak just like you. My American nephew would have been about your age. It is so sad, so ironic, so stupid. He was my sister's son, half American, half German. He joined the American army, and now lies dead in Normandy, killed by a German bullet."

She turned to Mutti. "There is something else I do not quite believe about this son of yours. I hear that he has asthma, and that is why he has been excused military service. But I have been watching him, and I have seen no sign of this asthma. In fact he looks to me to be strong as an ox. Hans believes he may be an enemy pilot, a bomber pilot, and I think he may be right. If he is, and you are caught, then we all know what will happen, not just to him, but to you also, all of you. I would not want to see that happen."

Mutti tried to interrupt, but the countess would not let her. "I think it is best that you should leave, and right away. You will have your reasons for doing what you are doing, and I am sure they are good reasons. But I do not want to know them. The less I know, the better. Your little boy looks to me as if he is quite well enough to travel now. Once Hans has alerted the police, they will not take long to get here, that is for sure. So I think you should go tonight, now, before it is too late. I shall of course tell the police that I am sure Hans's suspicions are quite groundless. But when you go, if you do not mind, I should like you to do something for me, something that is very important. I want you to take those children with you, the choir. They have no one to look after them any more. Their

choirmaster was killed, and several of the children too, on their way here. I want you to let them travel with you, to look after them. Would you do that? I know it is a lot to ask. But I have seen how much they love that elephant of yours. They will go willingly with you. They will go where she goes. I cannot keep them here for ever. I should like to, but I just do not have the room. As you can see, I am overcrowded as it is, and more come every day. I will give you enough food, for you and for them, to get you on your way."

She spoke in English now, to Peter, and looking him in the eye. "Tell me the truth now, young man. Am I right? Are you what I think you are? American?"

"Canadian," Peter replied. "RAF."

"I was close enough then," she said, in German again. "This war is coming to an end very soon. I think the Americans must be very close now. It will all be over, but too late for my husband, sadly. And since I know your truth, I will tell you mine. A few months ago my husband took part in a plot to assassinate Hitler. My husband was a good German, a good officer who believed we had been led down the wrong road, a terrible road into this war, and he just wanted it to stop. The only way to do it, he thought, was to kill Hitler. So he and his friends tried to do it, tried to end the suffering. They failed, and he died for what he believed in. I believe what he believed, that the suffering must end. This is why I am doing what I do now. This is why your secret will be my secret. So gather your things and come downstairs, but hurry. I have already assembled the children, and have given each one of them enough food for a few days. It is all I can spare. Be quick now. The further you are gone from here before dawn the better."

She left us then, before Mutti or any of us could say a word of thanks.

We dressed quickly, gathered our things, and made our way downstairs. The children were all waiting in the hall, the countess too. We were saying our goodbyes when the front door opened, and Hans came in. He was not alone. He had an army officer with him, and several soldiers, their rifles pointing right at us.

3.

THE OFFICER SALUTED. "COUNTESS, PLEASE FORGIVE this intrusion, but I have come—"

"Major Klug," the countess said, advancing towards him and proffering her hand. "How good to see you again. I know why you have come. I think perhaps we should talk privately, don't you? But first, perhaps... your soldiers, their rifles, they are frightening the children."

The major hesitated. He seemed at a loss for a moment as to how to deal with the situation. But he recovered quickly enough. "Very well, Countess, if you insist." He ordered the soldiers to lower their weapons, told us all to stay right where we were, then

followed the countess into her study.

I do not know how long we stood there in the hallway, waiting, but it seemed like a lifetime. No one spoke. All the while I held Peter's hand, knowing these might be the last moments we would have together. Karli kept looking up at Mutti, his eyes filled with tears.

But Mutti did not notice. Like all of us, she was straining to listen, to make some sense out of the murmur of voices we could all hear on the other side of that door.

When at last the door opened the major came out on his own. Without a glance at any of us, without a word, he strode swiftly across the hall towards the front door. He waited for a moment for a bewildered Hans to open it for him, and then left, his soldiers following him. The countess came out moments later, a glass in her hand. She was breathing quite heavily. "I am afraid I had to have a little drink," she said, "to stop myself shaking." She smiled at us then. "Do not look so worried. Actually I think it all went quite well, better than I could have hoped for. It was lucky for us that it was Major Klug who came. He served with my husband in the same regiment. They knew each other quite well. Anyway, it is all over now. In the sense in which we needed him to be, he is, I am sure, an honourable man. He will keep his word. You are safe to go."

"What do you mean?" Mutti asked her. "What did he say? What did you tell him?"

"You have heard of the stick and the carrot?" the countess went on. "When you want to persuade someone to do something they do not wish to do, you need both, don't you? Stick and carrot. First, I used the stick. I reminded him that the Americans are maybe no more than a week or two away, that if anything happened to any of you, I personally would see to it that when they come the Americans would know Major Klug was responsible, and that I would make quite sure he was shot. As for the carrot, I keep some money in my safe, not much, but it helped. And just to be sure, I read him a few words from my husband's last letter from prison before they executed him – Major Klug had great respect for my husband. My husband wrote – and I know the words by heart –

It makes me happy to know that out of the ashes of this horror, a new Germany must grow, and that you, and our friends and family will be a part of it. Remember always

the words of Goethe that I love: 'Whatever you can do, begin it. Boldness has genius, power and magic. Begin it now.' So, begin the new Germany, my darling, help it grow. I know you will. I am sad I will not be there to see it in person, but I shall always be with you in spirit.

Major Klug seemed to take this very much to heart, as I hoped he would."

When the time came to leave later that same night, the countess kissed Karli and told him to behave himself, and then we were walking away from the house. By the time I turned to look she had gone inside. Following along behind us were the choir-school children, in pairs, a sack on every back, and as silent as we were, Mutti walking with them. Peter went on ahead, our pathfinder as usual, while I led Marlene, with Karli riding up on her, all of us knowing we owed our lives to that extraordinary and wonderful lady.

It was hard to leave the warmth and comfort of the house behind us, and be out there again, walking

through the cold of the night. It took me a while to get used to the discomfort, and the tiredness. In a way, the school children must have helped. They were a diversion, I suppose. I had little time now to worry about myself. Travelling was slower with them, of course.

But we managed somehow to keep going. For the most part it was Mutti and I who did our best to look after the choir-school children, strictly rationing the food the countess had given us, keeping them cheerful, encouraging and comforting them through their exhaustion and their fear and sorrow. But I am sure it was Marlene who was the saving of them because Marlene made them laugh. They loved to watch her splashing in the streams, loved to feed her by hand whenever they could, and, like Karli, loved to have a good giggle whenever they heard her... how can I say this politely?... letting off – which was often, and it was very smelly too!

Karli grew up fast during those days and nights of hardship. There was no more showing off. I think maybe the compass incident, the disaster he had so nearly brought upon us that day, had changed him, made him more aware of other people. It was Karli's idea, for instance, that two of the choir-school children should take it in turns to ride up with him on Marlene, one in front of him, one behind. It was the best of ideas because it gave them all something to look forward to, and that was so important. It kept their spirits up, and ours too, come to that because it was so heartening to see the children enjoying themselves.

It was not long, of course, before our supply of

food ran out. For Peter, after that, it was like the feeding of the five thousand, only he was no miracle worker. Whatever food he would bring back from his scavenging missions into the countryside, from his dawn raids on farmsteads, had to be divided up between us all, and all too often there was very little to divide up. He told me he was having to take ever greater risks when it came to stealing food for us, and that dogs were his worst enemy. Once, he was even shot at from an upstairs window. He had broken into some isolated farmhouse, and was grabbing what he could from the kitchen, when the farmer's dog attacked him, baying and barking like a wild thing. He had to drop everything and run. Luckily, the farmer did not shoot straight, but the dog managed to sink his teeth into Peter's ankle, and that pained him for days afterwards.

With the snow gone, early signs of spring were all around us by now, the trees budding, the meadows and hedgerows dotted with flowers. And the birds sang. But there was rain, and often at night too. We trudged on, through fields and forests, fording streams where we had to, following Peter, following his compass. But from those last weeks of our long journey into the night, I do not remember so much the tiredness, nor the cold and the wet, nor the aching hunger we were all living with the whole time now. What I remember best was the children singing. I think it probably started as one of Mutti's ideas to keep them happy, to keep their minds occupied. And once they began singing they did not seem to want to stop. They sang, as we marched along, lightening the darkness for all of us. They sang, crammed together in some shepherd's hut, in some forester's shed, huddling together for warmth. And when they sang, sooner or later we joined in. We loved that, loved being part of their music-making. We were singing away our fears, and doing it together.

We must have been a strange sight for those who caught sight of us: Peter and I, stomping along together ahead, an elephant behind us with two or three children aboard, and, following them, Mutti and her cavalcade of singing children. Karli was getting on

so well with the other children by now, that often he would get down off Marlene and walk along with them, singing with them. I think he did not want to be left out, he wanted to feel he was one of them. It would not be true to say that all this singing meant we could entirely forget our discomforts, our hunger and our anxieties, but it most certainly helped us to put one foot in front of the other.

As the days and nights passed, there was something else that lifted our spirits, and gave us new hope. We were no longer hearing the sound of guns behind us. They were ahead of us now, lighting the western horizon every night – American artillery, Peter told us. That put a real spring in our step, but at the same time we knew that no guns were friendly guns, even if they were American. We were still in grave danger.

More often than not now, we found ourselves sharing whatever shelter we could find with other refugees, and often with dozens of retreating German soldiers too, which made us all very nervous. But we need not have worried. They were all far too exhausted, and too depressed, to ask questions. They all loved to make a fuss of Marlene, and I think it helped also to have the children with us. Even the soldiers seemed happy to share what little food they had. It is true also that once or twice, someone did steal our food whilst we were sleeping – but then it would be fair to say that Peter had stolen it in the first place, I suppose.

Peter made himself very popular with everyone because whenever he came back from one of his successful scrounging quests, he would share out all he could. The soldiers we encountered came with their stories like everyone else, and all their stories told one tale, that Americans were very close now, that they were breaking through everywhere, that their armies could be just over the next hill.

But it still came as a surprise to us on that day we first met up with the Americans. We were late finding our shelter that morning, but Peter was not too worried because there was a thick mist all around us, and we were well enough hidden. But of course that

made it all the more difficult to spot a likely barn or shed where we could lie up for the day.

I remember we were making our way up a hillside, the early morning mists thinner now and wispier than before. All the children were singing, Karli too, walking along with them. I was leading Marlene by the ear, talking to her, as I often did, when she suddenly stopped, and lifted her head. Ahead of us, Peter had stopped too, and was holding up his hand. For just a moment or two, I thought he had found us a shelter, but I couldn't see it. There was no barn, no shed, only trunkless trees rising strangely out of the mist. The children had fallen silent. We all stood there, bewildered at the terrifying crescendo of sound we were now hearing. It seemed to be coming from all around us, roaring, rattling, creaking, clanking, and it was coming closer all the time. The ground itself was shaking under our feet.

Then out through the mist they came. Tanks! Twenty or thirty of them, and they kept on coming. "Americans!" Peter shouted. "They are Americans!"

And he began waving at them frantically, and running towards them. That was when Marlene took fright. She pulled away from me, and fled. I went after her, calling and calling for her to come back. But her run became a charging stampede. Trumpeting in her terror, her ears flapping wildly, her trunk flailing, she simply disappeared into the mist.

By the time the lead tank reached us, they had all lurched to a stop. A soldier's head came up out of the turret. He pulled off his headphones, and stared at us in disbelief. I shall never forget the first words he said to us. "Holy cow! What in hell's name was that? Was that an elephant?"

"It was," Peter told him. "We sure are glad to see you."

"You American?" the soldier asked.

"Canadian." Peter replied. "RAF. Flight Sergeant Peter Kamm. Navigator. Shot down over Dresden a few weeks back."

"You walked all the way from Dresden?" the soldier asked, still incredulous. "With an elephant, and all those kids?"

"Yep," said Peter.

"Holy Cow!" the soldier said. "Well I'll be goddamned."

"We have to find that elephant," Peter told him. "We have to go after her. She has been with us all the way."

"Don't you worry," the soldier assured us cheerily. "We will find her for you. Nowhere much an elephant can go without being noticed, I'd say. But right now you guys have got to get out of here. There is a war going on, you know."

Mutti tried to argue with him, to let her go after Marlene. Karli and I begged him too. Mutti told him and told him that Marlene would just keep on running, that she would be terrified, that no one would be able

to catch her, except one of us. She knew only us, she trusted only us. But the soldier would not listen. We were all led away, still protesting, by an escort of soldiers. Mutti was inconsolable. I think she knew then that she would never see Marlene again. So at the moment of our greatest triumph, we had lost Marlene. For days, for weeks, we never stopped looking for her, asking after her. But no one had seen her. It was as if she had simply disappeared off the face of the earth."

At this point in the story Lizzie stopped, and looked at us as if to say: That's it, that's the end.

"And? And? What happened?" Karl was echoing my thoughts exactly. "What happened after that? To Marlene, to all of you? Did you find her in the end? And Papi, did Papi come home?"

"What happened afterwards?" Lizzie replied. "Oh, a lot happened, a whole lifetime of happenings. But I think I shall keep it short. I am suddenly rather tired. And you must be too. Well, here is how the story ends..."

"Within a day or two of meeting the Americans, we found ourselves – Mutti, Karli, me and the choir-school children – in a camp, a sort of refugee camp, for 'displaced persons', that was what they called us. Peter did all he could to stop them taking us away. He told them how Mutti had helped him to escape, told them the whole story. But rules were rules, they said, and that was that. All displaced Germans were being gathered up into camps.

Before we were loaded up and driven away in an army lorry, they gave us a few moments to say goodbye to him. That was when he pressed this compass into my hand, and told us that he promised he would go on looking for Marlene. Mutti was there, so was Karli, but I remember I could not help myself. When it came to my turn to say goodbye, I clung to him and cried. He whispered in my ear that he would write, that he

would come back for me and find me. The last I saw of him as we were driven away, he was standing there in the rain, in his uniform again now, waving us off. I thought my heart would break.

We all lived for six months or more in that camp. When I think about it now, it was not so bad, I suppose. There was no privacy, none, that was the worst of it. And I hated living behind barbed wire, unable to go where I wanted, do what I wanted. The huts were overcrowded, but they were warm and dry at night. Defeat was a bitter blow to many of the soldiers and refugees, but for our family I have to say that the end of the war and the death of Hitler came as a great relief. We learned that life goes on.

Amongst the thousands of prisoners there were many musicians and actors and poets. They produced plays, gave concerts. It broke the tedium of captivity. For an hour or two we could simply forget everything. The best concert for me, without any doubt, was when the choir-school children gave a performance for everyone. They sang mostly the folksongs we had sung together through those long nights tramping through the dark. They knew our family favourite was, 'I walked through a green forest'. I was quite sure, and so was Mutti and Karli, that they sang it specially for us.

Mutti decided after a while that what was needed in the camp was a school for all the children, including the choir-school children, and she needed my help, she said, to look after *die Kleine*, the little ones. It kept us both busy, and feeling useful too, and that was so important. Most important of all though to me in my time in the camp were the letters I got from Peter. I always wrote back the same day, to some address in London. He was always full of good news, and great plans, about how once things had settled down, and he could get leave, he would come back and fetch me. We were going to get married,

and then live in Canada together. We would go canoeing and fishing. He could not wait to show me the salmon and the black bears, and everything in the Canadian wilderness that he had told me so much about.

When we were all at last released from the camp, we had to say goodbye to the choir-school children. It was a tearful parting. They had become almost like family to us. The authorities only let us out because we had an address to go to. Mutti took us to live with a cousin of hers in Heidelberg. We had one room overlooking the river, where we could see the sun setting over the town. Renate was Mutti's oldest cousin, a school teacher and a bit strict and prim. She did her best to be kind to us, and tolerant, but she was used to living alone, and sometimes, I think, she found it difficult to hide her irritation with us.

Even though we were now free, and life was returning to some kind of normality, this was the worst time of all for me because Peter's letters just stopped coming. I had sent him our new address, but he never wrote again. And Mutti too was as unhappy as I had ever seen her. Every day she went to ask the authorities for news of Papi. There was none. Both the men we loved had disappeared. I am sure this was why I became closer during these days to Mutti than ever before.

And Karli? Poor Karli cried every night for Papi and Marlene, but he got on much better than either Mutti or me with Renate, and would tell her again and again all his stories about Marlene and our miraculous escape across Germany. In the end we managed to find ourselves a little apartment nearby. Renate arranged for Mutti to teach at her school, and found places there too for Karli and me. So we went back to school. It seemed strange to be back at school again after so much had happened. I was so full of sadness by now that I found studying impossible.

But then came the glad, glad news that Papi was alive. He had been taken prisoner by the

Russians over a year before. We did not know when he would be home, but he was alive and that was all that mattered. We cried for joy when we heard, and Mutti sat us round the table for a 'family moment'. Now I knew that Papi was safe, I prayed only for Peter. Every time the postman came, I would run out to meet him and ask if there was a letter. I kept writing, kept begging him to write back. But no letter came. I began to give up all hope of seeing him again.

Then one afternoon – it was a few months later – we were on our way back from school, and had just turned the corner into our street, when we saw there was someone sitting on our front doorstep, with a suitcase beside him. He stood up and took off his hat. It was Peter. The trouble was I had to share the hugging with Mutti and Karli.

"Why didn't you write?" I cried, not that it mattered now. Peter told me later that when he had left England and gone back to Canada, they just had not sent my letters on. Then they had all turned up one day at his home address in Canada in one big parcel. That was how he knew where to find us.

Maybe you have guessed the rest. We got married, in Heidelberg it was. You should have heard the bells ring out. A week or so later the two of us sailed for Canada. I hated to leave Mutti and Karli, but Mutti insisted.

"We have very few chances for happiness in this life," she said. "You take it. Go." Karli told me, as he said goodbye, that he would come and live in Canada when he was older, and he did too.

Sometimes all really is well that ends well.

It took another four years though before Papi finally came home from Russia. Mutti wrote that he was thin, but that she was feeding him up, and that as soon as he was well enough they were going to apply for visas to come to Canada and join us in our little town not far from Toronto. So that is how we all of us came to live here in Niagara-on-the-Lake. Peter was acting in the theatre here, and getting bigger parts all the time. And I became a nurse, like your mother, Karli. Life was good. Cold in winter, but good. Peaceful. Contented.

But that is not quite the end of it. One summer evening – we would have been in our forties now I suppose – Peter and I went to the circus in Toronto, a travelling circus from France. Peter always loved to watch clowning. He had a clown costume himself, and he would perform at children's parties sometimes. But right away it was not the clowns that interested me. The star of the show was an elephant, and I knew as soon as I set eyes on her that it was Marlene. And the extraordinary thing was that she knew me. As she was led around the ring in the grand parade, she stopped right by me where I was sitting in the front row, and reached out her trunk towards me. I felt her breath on me. I looked into her weepy eye. It was her. There was no doubt about it.

We went round the back afterwards, and talked to the circus people. They had bought her from another circus ten years before. They had no idea where she had come from before that. They said she was the best elephant they had ever had, that she had quite a sense of humour. I told them our whole story then. They cried, and we cried.

We spent long hours with her for the whole of that weekend, just talking to her, telling her about our lives, how Mutti and Papi had passed away within months of each other a while ago now, and how Karli was making films, how he could still do his juggling. The morning the circus was packing up to leave town, we were there to wave her off. We cried again, of course we did, but at the same time, we were not sad at all, just happy that we had met up again, that she had survived as we had, and that all was well with her.

I have been on my own for a while now, the

only one left. Peter and I were married for almost sixty years. I cannot say we never had a cross word. We had our problems and our sadnesses too. Everyone does. No children. I should have liked children of my own. But we were as happy as anyone has the right to be happy. And this is Peter's compass."

Lizzie held the compass out to Karl. "Yours now, Karli," she said.

I tried to protest, but she put it in Karl's hand and folded his fingers over it. "You keep it," she said. "You look after it, and look after my story too. I should like people to know about it. Oh, and do not forget to bring me my photograph album tomorrow, will you?"

I could see she was completely exhausted. I think she was asleep before we left her.

When I came to work the next morning – school had been cancelled because of the snow – Karl was

with me. We had Lizzie's photograph album with us. We sat on either side of her bed while she talked us through her photos, one or two of the family down on the farm, one of her wedding day in Heidelberg, some of Peter in theatrical costumes, several of them both, then in the new city of Dresden.

"And look!" she said, turning triumphantly to the last page. "This is Marlene and me at the circus that day! Do you believe me now?"

"I have always believed you," Karl told her.

"Always?"

"Always," said Karl.

"And you?" Lizzie asked, looking at me knowingly.

"Almost always," I replied.